April 18, 2016

To John,

Pat Maxwell

When Rain Comes

- A Sweet Historical Romance -

Patricia G. Maxwell

Acknowledgements

Writers are often portrayed as people closeted in an isolated spot creating works all on their own. The truth is, none of us works alone. Countless people walk beside us and help us. My special thanks to these folk who have helped me create this novel:

My husband, Burton Maxwell—the first reader of everything I write—always applauds my efforts. Thank you for a lifetime of encouragement. Our research-minded son, Daniel, kept me checking historical facts. Our marketing par excellence daughter, Pat, always says "you can do it, Mom!" Thanks, children, for your support.

My writing group: Louise Goodman, Sam Halpern, Annette Winter, Elsie Zala. You have been invaluable teachers of writing skills, kind critics, and wonderful friends. Thank you!

Thanks to friends and relatives who read early drafts and gave invaluable suggestions: Pat Curtis, Roberta Huston, Caroline Melville, Sharon Quinn, Gloria Reyna, Kathy Simpson. You helped immensely to sharpen the story and make it better.

Finally, I offer thanks to Nick from FirstEditing, who did a first-class job of cleaning up my grammar and punctuation. The fine folk at BookBaby did all the technical stuff to birth this baby into the E-book world and also put it into print copies. Thanks for your expertise.

Foreword

When my husband and I moved to the San Diego area eighteen years ago, we visited all the tourist spots. In Old Town I found a book about local history and started laughing over the tale of Charles Hatfield, a rainmaker hired by the city in 1915 to end a four-year drought. Nineteen inches of rain fell in the next three weeks creating devastating floods, the collapse of a dam, the loss of lives. People threatened to sue the city. Others wanted to run Mr. Hatfield out of town for doing his job too well.

It was a crazy, humorous, bizarre and awful event that gripped my attention. The more I delved into the story, the more it needed to be told from the standpoint of ordinary people living ordinary lives. There are books, videos, articles and a master's thesis about Mr. Hatfield, but I kept imagining what it would be like to hear from characters who lived through the events.

That's when it occurred to me to create some people, place them in the small town of Chula Vista, next door to the Lower Otay Dam which collapsed, and imagine what they would think, say and do. In other words, a novel was born out of actual, historical events, peopled by fictitious persons. Even more intriguing, would be to set a love story against the true-life disasters of those turbulent times.

When Rain Comes is the result of my playing with fascinating facts from a century ago.

Chapter One

It was mid-afternoon on August 23, 1915 when the trolley, known to locals as the "electric train," pulled into the Chula Vista, California station. Carrie looked out the window at a few scattered buildings lining an unpaved street. Beyond the sparse business district, lemon orchards stretched in every direction, houses scattered among them. She noticed utility poles and felt relieved that at least part of the town had electricity.

As the train slowed, three passengers rose from their seats and walked towards the exit. Carrie stood, gathered her tapestry valise from the empty seat next to her, looped the handles of her purse over her arm and moved down the aisle, smoothing her skirt as she walked. The train stopped, doors opened and people scurried out. A conductor stretched out his hand and helped her down the steps.

The warm afternoon air hit her in the face and her nostrils breathed in dust and heat. She looked around. The train depot, if you could call it that, looked no bigger than one room. Next door to the depot, a larger building stood with a diagonal sign advertising it as Farrow's General Store. One of the passengers entered the store. The other two crossed the street, hurrying toward familiar destinations. Homes. Families. Work places.

Tightness filled Carrie's throat. She swallowed hard and looked back at the train.

"Your trunk'll be off in a minute, ma'am. We'll set it there in the alcove." The conductor and another man, one on either end of her trunk, inched their feet down the steps of the trolley. Minutes later, they set the trunk against the wall of the depot and wiped their foreheads with the backs of their hands. "Delivery man'll be along shortly," the conductor said. "To take it to your destination."

"Thank you."

Minutes later, the two men swung themselves up into the car. The trolley pulled away, leaving Carrie standing alone. Pulling a handkerchief out of her skirt pocket she dabbed the perspiration on her nose and the moisture in her eyes and blinked a couple of times. She tucked a few stray hairs under her straw cloche hat, fingered the locket she always wore and studied her surroundings. Across the street on a corner, the signs on a two-story building read "Chula Vista State Bank," "E. Melville Realty Company," "Bakery," and "Millinery." Looking right, then left, she estimated town to be no more than two blocks in either direction.

The rattle of an engine got her attention and she turned toward the sound. A dusty truck sped down the street toward her and stopped abruptly. A tall, young man unfolded himself from the vehicle, stood and looked her direction. "Hello! You're the new teacher I'm picking up?"

He moved quickly and efficiently, circling the front end of the truck and coming her way all in one seamless action. He wore khaki pants and a long-sleeved blue shirt rolled up to his elbows revealing deeply tanned arms. Short, brown hair, with a hint of a wave on top was brushed back from his forehead. A smile spread across his clean-shaven face making his brown eyes sparkle.

He extended his hand. "Nathan Landon. Everybody calls me Nate."

She offered her hand, the warmth and strength of his filtering through the fabric of her glove, startling in how good it felt. "Carolyn Wyngate. Everybody calls me Carrie."

Nate smiled. "Welcome to the lemon capitol of the world. You're staying where?"

"I'm renting a room from the Owenses. 525 F Street."

"That's close by. I'll have you there in minutes."

"Good. I'm ready to stop traveling."

"Where'd you come from?"

"Chicago."

"Chicago! That's quite a ways."

Nate bent over her trunk and lifted it so easily it amazed her. Carrying it to the pickup, he put it in, then wiped his hands on his pants as he returned to where she stood.

"Let me help you into the truck." He opened the door and placed his hand under her elbow, guiding her into the passenger seat. She settled herself and adjusted her hat as he rounded the truck, opened his door and slid in.

Glancing her way, he said, "I'm afraid my truck is no match to the taxis you're probably used to. My other job is with a lemon orchard. A truck comes in handy when working the land."

"We used public transportation most the time in Chicago."

"We?"

"My grandmother and I."

"No parents?"

"Both died when I was young. Grandma raised me." Carrie squirmed against the seat and twisted the cloth handles of her purse between her fingers. Untwisted them. "Have you always lived here?"

"Our family moved out from Kansas when I was ten. Great place to grow up. Fishing in the bay. Playing on the beach. Riding the train to San Diego. Catching the ferry to Coronado on weekends."

Nate put the truck in gear and edged it away from the train stop. "Say, why don't I give you a tour of the area? Since you're new here." He turned his head toward her. She focused her eyes on the hood of the truck and set her mouth in a tight line. She twined her fingers together and squeezed them. Hard.

"Is that part of your job?"

"No. A personal offer."

"Sorry. I can't accept."

Jerking his head toward her, eyebrows scrunched together, he stammered, "Forgive me. I didn't mean to be indiscreet."

With a quick glance in his direction, Carrie saw that the twinkle had gone out of his eyes. She dropped her head and stared at her hands. "You should work for the Chamber of Commerce, Nate."

"Would that make my offer acceptable?" He returned his gaze to the street ahead, turning the truck to the right onto F Street.

"I'm not sure. Perhaps we should consult an etiquette book."

The corners of Nate's mouth lifted slightly, though he didn't say anything. A block down F Street, he pointed right. "There's the school building. You're lucky to teach in a brand new school."

A long, white, one-story concrete structure took up half a block. Six sections of tall windows faced the street, three on either side of an entry with two pillars. A circular drive led to the building.

Nate continued his commentary. "You know, of course, that all we have in Chula Vista is an elementary school. After eighth grade, students ride the electric train into San Diego to attend high school."

"No. I didn't know. That's what you did?"

"Yep. Up every morning at 5 a.m. to milk the cows before hopping on the train. I liked high school. A chance to mingle with more students than we had here."

Nate paused as he braked the truck for a hen and rooster crossing the dirt street in front of them. "You probably had good-sized schools in Chicago."

"It's not size that makes a good school."

"You don't think so? What is it?"

"Inspiring teachers. That's what I want to be."

"I bet you are already."

"I've taught for two years."

"Really? Then we're getting an experienced teacher for our school." He turned toward her with a grin.

Carrie mumbled "I hope so."

Nate leaned one arm out the side window as he continued driving west on F Street. He didn't say anything more for a few minutes. He slowed the truck and parked in front of a path that led to a two-story, white house with a porch on the front corner.

"You'll like boarding with the Owenses. They're really nice people. He's a barber. She's a fabulous cook. Has a way with flowers, too."

A bed of marigolds, snapdragons and daisies occupied the space below three tall windows centered on the front wall of the house. To the right of the windows, steps led to the front porch that housed a couple of rocking chairs. It looked inviting.

Nate parked the truck and got out, came around to her door and opened it. Taking her hand, he helped her step down from the truck until she stood inches in front of him. Their eyes met briefly, then she looked away. He stepped to the back of the truck and lifted out the trunk. "I'll follow you," he said.

Carrie walked up the front path, Nate behind her. She had barely stepped onto the front porch when the door opened and a plump lady with a happy face stepped out. Her smile stretched from one round cheek to the other. "Oh! You must be Carolyn Wyngate! We've been waiting for you! Come in!"

"Hello, Mrs. Owens."

"You needn't call me Mrs. Owens. My name's Bertie. Everybody calls me Aunt Bertie."

"Alright, Aunt Bertie."

The older woman held the door open and Carrie entered, followed by Nate, carrying the trunk.

"Nate, you can take the trunk on up the stairs. First door to the right. Come on, Carrie, let me show you your room."

The two women followed Nate up the stairs, entering the room as he set the trunk down on an oval-shaped braided rug.

Carrie looked around. A big window faced east, covered with white, lace curtains. She'd pull them back to let in more light and air. On the opposite wall, a single bed stood with a lavender quilt on it. Her favorite color. A chest of drawers stood along a side wall. Next to the window was a small desk. She'd move it directly in front of the window.

Nate turned toward the door, and Carrie reached in her handbag for money to pay him. He shook his head. "Train company pays me for doing deliveries."

Giving Carrie a sidewise glance, he said, "This has been a special delivery. Isn't every day I get to bring an inspiring teacher into our community."

Carrie felt her face grow hot, then her insides churned. Flattery. It won't work with me. Nate stepped out the door and descended the stairs, Carrie following him to the front porch.

"Thank you, Nate."

"You're welcome." He gave her a sly grin. "Due to the size of this city, I'm sure we'll meet again."

She watched him walk away from her, head high, shoulders broad and stride long. When he reached the truck, he waved at her over the roof of the vehicle, ducked into his seat and started whistling.

"Such a nice young man," a voice from behind said. It was Bertie, who stood in the front doorway. "Always cheerful."

"Does he always whistle?"

"Guess so." Bertie laughed. "You must be tired. Why don't you sit down while I get us some lemonade." Bertie motioned to a rocking chair, and Carrie sank into it as the older woman disappeared into the house. A few minutes later, she returned, carrying a tray with two glasses of lemonade and a plate of cookies. Carrie took a glass and sipped the cool liquid. So refreshing.

"I can't wait for my husband, Archie, to come home from work. He owns a barbershop on Third Avenue. He's going to like you, and I'm sure you'll like him. He's such a kind man. I don't know how I was so lucky to catch him."

There was warmth and love in Bertie's voice.

"Must be nice to find the right man."

"It is. You'll find it one day, too, Honey."

"Right now I'm focusing on being a good teacher. It's an honor the school board picked me. I don't want to let them down."

"I'm sure you won't. You'll probably have a harder time living up to your own expectations."

"Maybe. But I've got to. It's the only way to get anywhere."

Bertie stirred her lemonade, the spoon tinkling against the edge of the glass. She leaned into her chair and said nothing for several minutes, then changed the subject by stating, "We always have breakfast at seven in the morning, dinner at six. You'll be taking a lunch to school, I presume. Anyway, it's time for me to get into the kitchen and work on dinner."

"May I help?"

"Not today. Get yourself unpacked and settled into your room. There'll be plenty of other times when you can help."

Carrie drained her glass of lemonade and set the empty glass back on the tray, then stood. "It won't take me long to unpack. I'll probably still have time to help with dinner."

She turned toward the stairs and ascended them quickly, then ducked into her room, and set about unpacking her trunk as quickly as possible. The last item in the trunk was a photograph of her and her grandmother. Placing it on the chest of drawers, Carrie whispered "Well, I'm here, Grandma.

Chapter Two

A half block away from the Owenses' house, Nate stopped whistling. He slapped the steering wheel with the palm of his hand and muttered, "What a fool! First time you meet, you invite her for a drive." He tried to analyze the events of the last hour. His mind delivered only a picture of a petite young woman with hazel eyes and auburn hair that curled against her cheeks. Tiny dimples on either side of her mouth deepened when she smiled, which wasn't often. A serious person. Or maybe tired. Nervous? Afraid? After a long trip, who wouldn't be all of those things?

Nate clenched his teeth together. How stupid of me!

He was halfway home when he remembered the errands he was supposed to do: refill the digitalis prescription for his father at the drug store, buy a sack of beans at the general store for his mother and pick up a bag of grain at the feed store for the horse.

It took an hour due to the social aspect of doing business in a small town.

"How's your father?" Mr. Walsh, the pharmacist, asked.

"Fine. This medicine seems to be working well for him."

"Tell him to take it easy."

"That's like telling water to run up hill."

At the general store, two customers were discussing the weather. "The drought's been goin' on for nearly four years," a rancher from Otay valley said.

"Nothin' new," an old man in sagging overalls replied. "Always been dry spells here. Then, the rain comes. Sometimes too much."

Everybody in town knew that Nate did occasional delivery work for the railroad. This became a topic of conversation, especially if there was a scarcity of other news. It was not surprising when Pete, the owner of the feed store, asked, "Pick up anything interesting from the afternoon train?"

Nate stuck his hands in his pockets and raised his eyes to study the ceiling rafters. "H-m-m-m. Let's see." He leveled his eyes and looked at Pete. The man, with straw-dusted hair, stood with fingers looped into the bib of striped-blue overalls, mouth slightly open, bristly eyebrows lifted in an uneven arch.

"Well, what're you holdin' back on me?"

Nate laughed. "Nothing, Pete. I'm figuring in my head how long it will take for the news to get around town."

"Accusing me of being a gossip?"

"Not at all. This isn't gossip. It's news."

"So, what's the news?"

"A new school teacher has arrived in town."

"What's she like?"

"How could I know in the short time I was with her?"

"Sometimes you know something in here." Pete tapped a finger over his heart. "Before you know it up here." The finger moved to his forehead.

Nate shrugged his shoulders and didn't respond. After being advised, interrogated and prodded about romance from people around town, he chose silence to everyone's urgings.

"I need to be going, Pete. See you next time the horse gets hungry."

When he reached home, Nate parked the pickup close to the barn, unloaded the sack of feed and trudged toward the house, the faux pas with Carrie heavy on his mind. He dragged his feet toward the back porch.

As he climbed the steps, he started whistling. Opening the door, he stepped into the kitchen, where his mother stood at the table rolling out pie dough.

"You sound cheerful," she said without looking up. "As usual."

"Might as well be."

"Anything interesting today?"

"Picked up the new school teacher at the train stop. Delivered her to the Owenses', where she'll be boarding."

"Where's she coming from?"

"Chicago."

"We're becoming an important town to attract a teacher from Chicago."

"Looks like it."

With a scuffling of feet on the porch and a push against the door, Nate's father elbowed his way into the kitchen, carrying an armful of freshly husked corn.

"Found a few good ears for supper. Most the corn is dried up from too little water and too much heat."

Nate frowned. "I did my best to keep a regular watering schedule."

"I know you did, Son. It's not your fault. You've done a good job of portioning out the water."

"Maybe I should have put less on the lemon trees and more on the garden."

"Don't think it would've made much difference. Besides, your mom and I want you to get as much of a harvest off those trees as possible."

"Thanks, Dad."

The evening had been pleasant. Mr. Owens came home from his barbershop and was introduced to Carrie. She immediately liked him. He was what she imagined her father would have been if he hadn't been taken from her. Mr. Owens was a man of average height with dark brown hair beginning to gray at the edges and brown eyes that had a friendly warmth to them. During dinner, he conversed with Carrie about her goals as a teacher. He and his wife, Bertie, both seemed interested in her thoughts and listened well as she explained how her grandmother had instilled in her a love of learning.

"Grandma took me to the public library every week, where we both checked out armloads of books. She took me to museums, art galleries, and concerts, opening my eyes to the whole world."

Carrie paused in amazement that she'd kept tears out of her voice and eyes when speaking of her grandmother.

Mr. Owens set his fork on the edge of his plate and said, "We don't have museums and art galleries here yet, but we will. Right now, we're working on a library."

"There's no library here? I don't know how I can live without a library!"

Immediately, Carrie felt she had spoken out of turn. "I'm sorry. I didn't mean it to come out like that."

Mr. Owens chuckled. "It's all right. I know how you feel. I love to read, too. We're not totally without a library. A group of citizens donated books and opened a reading room staffed by volunteers."

"So, a start has been made."

"That's not all. Earlier this year, the city hired a part-time librarian. They've also requested a Carnegie library grant. It looks like we'll get it."

"Oh, good," Carrie replied. "I like to encourage students to visit the library and learn to enjoy all kinds of books."

Bertie stood and started removing dishes from the table. "It sounds like we're blessed to have you here as a teacher."

Carrie blushed and stammered. "I want to do my best. Education is so important. Here, let me help you with the dishes."

She rose from her chair and reached for a serving dish. Together, they cleared the table in two trips to the kitchen.

"There's lemon pie for dessert," Bertie announced. "That's one thing we have around here. Lots of lemons." She paused, then continued, "But if we don't get rain soon, we may not have so many. People are mighty worried."

Bertie lifted a pie out of the pie-keeper on the kitchen counter and began slicing three ample pieces and setting them on plates. She and Carrie carried them to the table along with three cups of coffee.

Mr. Owens smiled at his wife. "Looks like you've done it again." He turned toward Carrie. "Bertie makes the best lemon pies in town. She really ought to enter one into the county fair."

Carrie lifted her fork and took a bite. "Agreed. This is delicious."

As they ate, Carrie thought about the easy and comfortable way Mr. and Mrs. Owens interacted. They seemed to care a lot about each other. If I ever get married, this is the way I want it. She stopped that thought with another. Focus on teaching. Not marriage.

Bertie picked up her coffee cup. "Well, Archie, what's the news about town today?"

"They're reinstating telephones in City Hall."

Mr. Owens licked a fleck of meringue off his upper lip and explained "Two years ago Chula Vista nearly went broke. To save money, they took the phones out of City Hall."

Bertie stirred her coffee. "We've really had some bad times the last two years."

For the next few minutes, Mr. and Mrs. Owens reiterated recent history. The big freeze in 1913 had killed the new growth on many of the lemons, including most of their own orchard. After the freeze came unprecedented heat and drought. Mr. Owens summed up the recital of events by saying, "Things are beginning to turn around. Phones are back. New library coming."

"Then I've come at a good time," Carrie said and amended her remark by adding, "but I'm sorry for all the bad times you've had."

"In spite of the difficulties, we wouldn't live anywhere else," Mr. Owens said. "This is a beautiful place with lots of possibilities."

"I'm looking forward to getting acquainted with the community; but if you'll excuse me, I'd better get to bed soon."

"Oh, you poor dear," Bertie said. "You've had a long day, and we've been babbling away keeping you from your rest."

"I've enjoyed every minute," Carrie said. "Thank you for telling me about the area."

As Carrie mounted the stairs to her room, she thought how different Chula Vista was from Chicago. Pushing aside the curtains at the window, she stared into the darkness. Here and there, lights glowed in the windows of houses scattered far from each other. A dozen street lamps, like thin halos, marked the bounds of the two-block business district. There were no sounds of traffic. No voices from adjoining apartment stoops. Only stillness. And stars. Millions of them. Close enough to touch.

She stretched her arms toward them, inhaling deeply and exhaling slowly, promising to be a star for all the children who would sit in all her classrooms.

Chapter Three

Sunlight flooded Carrie's room the next morning as she had hoped it would when she pulled back the curtains the night before. Rising from her bed, she walked to the window and studied the view of lemon orchards below. The scene was so different from the one from her window in Chicago that it seemed she had traveled to a different planet. What had she been thinking to leave a city of two million to come to a town of less than a thousand? For a moment, Carrie felt a shockwave of panic. She fought it down by raising her chin and telling herself that today would be the beginning of a new life that she couldn't wait to start.

Fifteen minutes later, she entered the kitchen, where Bertie stood at the stove frying eggs. They exchanged greetings, and Carrie sat down at the table to a breakfast of coffee, toast and eggs. Bertie chatted about her husband, who had already left for work. "Says he has bookwork to do which he can never get done once he opens the doors and people come in."

Carrie nodded. "That's why I want to get into the classroom a few days ahead of time before the rush of students come in."

"I can see you're a very responsible young lady."

"Thank you, and thank you for breakfast."

It was less than a half mile walk to the new school. Carrie felt grateful to have lodging so close to her work. And the Owenses are nice people, she thought as she turned onto the circular drive that led to the front entry. A note was attached to one of the double doors. It read: "The school building is not open today. If anyone needs to speak with me, you'll find me at the old school building. Principal Jenkins"

Where is the old school? Carrie wondered as she retraced her steps down the circular drive and onto F Street. She walked another block to the center of town where she met a woman carrying a bag of groceries who pointed east. "It's that two-story building beyond the church."

Carrie crossed the street and hurried toward the old building. It had eight steps to the front porch and she had just reached the top one when a boy charged through the front door and straight at her. He swerved to miss her, but his arm bumped hers and unbalanced her. She stumbled and fell across the front porch, pain shooting through her ankle. Behind her, she heard the boy's footsteps retreating and a voice yelling, "Stop!" Then the voice, which sounded familiar, said, "Carrie!" She struggled to sit up and pull her foot out from under her. Nate knelt before her, his face inches from hers. "Are you all right?"

"I think I sprained my ankle."

They both looked at her ankle, where a purplish bump had already risen on one side.

"I'll help you into my truck and we'll get some medical help."

"Oh, no! I don't have time to be laid up. It's just a sprain. I'll rest a bit and be fine."

"I don't think so. Let me at least take you back to the Owenses."

"I can rest right here, and in a few minutes it'll be better."

"Try wiggling it for me."

Carrie started to rotate her ankle, but a new arrow of pain shot up her leg. "Guess I can't move it too well yet."

"I guess not. Now, I'm going to pick you up and carry you to my truck."

"Really, Nate. That's not necessary. Just support me a little and I can walk."

"All right. I'll help you up. You take my arm, and we'll walk you down the stairs."

He stood behind her, wrapped his arms around her, and lifted her to a standing position. Then he moved to her side and offered his arm. "Hang onto me, and we'll walk very slowly down the first step."

The pain in her ankle radiated all the way to her knee, making it impossible to put weight on the foot. She leaned into Nate, clutched his arm and half-shuffled, half-hopped down the step. Nate steadied her as they stood still for a moment.

"Hurts pretty bad?"

"Worse than I thought it would."

"We'll take it slowly. Don't worry, Carrie, I won't let you fall."

She gripped his arm tighter and said, "Let's try the next step."

It took several minutes to navigate down the steps to the path leading to the street. She kept the weight off her injured ankle and lurched toward Nate's vehicle with his support. When they reached the truck, he somehow hung onto her and opened the door at the same time. Before she had time to object, he swept her in his arms and set her on the seat. Smoothing her skirt with one hand to keep the edge of her petticoat from showing, she pulled her feet in slowly and tried to arrange the injured one so it wouldn't hurt. It didn't work. Turning her face away from Nate, Carrie bit her lip.

As he drove away from the school and toward the Owenses' house, she disguised her discomfort by summoning a calm voice and asking, "Where did you come from? I didn't hear your car."

"Perhaps you were too absorbed in your own thoughts."

"Probably. School plans."

"Looks like you'll have to set aside those plans for awhile."

Carrie groaned. "I can't. I've got to get off to a good start."

"Whew!" Nate exhaled.

She turned her head toward him. "What does that mean?"

"It means you're a very determined woman."

Carrie angled her body away from him and straightened her back against the seat. "I have to be."

"When we get to the Owenses', you sit right here while I go to the door and tell her what's happened and we can decide whether I should carry you upstairs or put you down somewhere else."

"Sounds like I'm one of your packages to be set in a particular spot."

Nate had parked the truck and climbed out of his seat. He leaned his head back through the window and said "Didn't say you were, but if I were to make the comparison, I'd say you're one of the best packages I've ever delivered."

His head disappeared before she could react, and she watched him stride around the front of the car and up the walkway to the Owenses' porch. His legs were long and his steps quick and sure. She saw the front door open, the two of them talking, then Mrs. Owens hurrying toward her, Nate following behind.

"Oh, Carrie, I'm so sorry! What a pity! On your first trip to the school! I told Nate to put you on the couch in the front room. We'll get ice on that ankle. I'll call for the doctor."

"No need for that, Aunt Bertie. I'm sure I'll mend quickly. Do you have something I can wrap around the ankle?"

"Nate and I'll fix you right up."

Carrie winced. The ankle throbbed. She wished Nate didn't have to help her anymore than to get her onto that couch. Within minutes, he had lifted her out of the truck in his arms and set her down carefully. She held the injured foot up, and they hopped forward, his arm supporting her. They took the steps slowly, crossed the porch, entered the house and walked across the living room. Carrie sat down on the couch, and Nate helped lift her legs onto it.

Bertie fussed with pillows until she had two or three piled behind Carrie. She leaned into them and let out a sigh.

"Thank you, Bertie. Thank you, Nate."

"He was your angel," Bertie said. "How else can you explain that he happened to drive by and see when you fell?"

Carrie chose not to reply to Bertie's angel idea. Nate didn't say anything either as he headed for the front door. After he left, Carrie replayed the accident in her mind as Bertie disappeared into the kitchen to make an ice pack for the injured ankle. She relived the feel of Nate's arms supporting her, then scooping her up so close that she could smell him—a clean, fresh soap smell. Another thing she couldn't dismiss was how safe she felt with Nate. In spite of her resistance, he stayed calm and focused on what needed to be done about her injury.

Bertie came in and placed an ice pack on her ankle, pulled an afghan over her body and said, "Now, you rest."

Suddenly, Carrie felt tired. She closed her eyes but kept seeing Nate's face in her mind. She opened them again. Quit fantasizing. Nate's a nice man who helped you. That's all. You don't want, or need, anything more than that.

She fell asleep trying to come up with ways to discourage Nate Landon. Or any other man, for that matter.

Chapter Four

Nate drove back to the school and entered the building looking for anyone who might have seen the boy who bumped into Carrie. He found the principal, Mr. Jenkins, dressed in overalls and a checkered shirt, in a classroom putting books into boxes. Mr. Jenkins got a strange look on his face as he listened to Nate tell the story about Carrie's accident.

"That was probably my son. He's the only one who's been around here this morning. My wife sent him down to bring me a lunch. That boy's always running everywhere he goes, and I'm always telling him to slow down. But for him to run away after he caused someone to fall, that's totally unacceptable."

"Maybe he didn't know that she fell."

"Doesn't matter. He caused someone to be injured. Guess I'll have to have a little session with him in the woodshed."

Before he had thought it through, Nate blurted, "I hope you'll get his side of the story before you take drastic action."

The muscles in Mr. Jenkins jawline tightened. "I don't need anybody telling me how to discipline my children."

"I didn't mean to interfere in any way. By the way, how old is your son?"

"Nine."

"A fourth grader, perhaps?"

"I'm very aware that was his new teacher he ran into, but you stay out of this. I'll take care of it."

"Yes, sir. I'm on my way to the hardware store, so goodbye, Mr. Jenkins."

As Nate drove to the store, he considered Mr. Jenkins' words and attitude. It made him uneasy. First for the boy; then for Carrie. She'd be working in a school for a man who sounded hard and exacting. Nate was sure that Carrie's ideals of being an inspiring teacher would clash with Mr. Jenkins' methods.

Carrie. She seemed to be everywhere inside and outside of his head. Why had he happened to drive by the old school this morning just as she fell? He knew she was hurt the minute he saw her biting her lips and squeezing her eyes shut.

What he hadn't been prepared for were the feelings that surfaced when he carried her close to him. It reminded him of when he was six years old and rescued a baby bird fallen from its nest. He held it so carefully his fingers ached. He wanted it to be alright. Just like he wanted Carrie to be alright, because she mattered to him.

As Nate parked the truck in front of the hardware store, he frowned. Only two meetings with the woman and she matters to me? I bet I don't matter to her.

He got out of the truck, squared his shoulders and walked toward the store. When he opened the door, a voice called out: "Hello, Nate!"

"Hello, Mr. Shafer. Came by to pick up some nails for building a fence and some door hinges to repair the barn."

"Building a fence?"

"Yep. 'Good fences make good neighbors,' is what Robert Frost said."

Mr. Shafer laughed. "Nothing like a little poetry early in the morning in a hardware store. Then again, I shouldn't be surprised. You were a bit of the scholarly type in high school. I figured you'd be going off to college, but you've stayed around to be a farmer."

"Maybe I'll still get there one day. Used to think I'd like to go to agricultural college."

"That'd be nice. On the other hand, you might learn as much by talking with the Japanese farmers around here. I hear some of them have quit growing lemons and gone to growing celery."

"Maybe they're on to something, but how can I chat with them? I don't speak Japanese."

The two men kept talking as Mr. Shafer gathered Nate's supplies and rang them up.

Nate dug in his pocket for money and plunked it on the counter. "It's sure handy Mike's lumber yard is next door. Got to go there next for the fence posts."

Minutes later, Nate was selecting fence posts, and Mike was helping load them into the truck. Nate planned to head straight home and begin work on the fence but had a sudden idea. He drove to the pharmacy instead.

"Mr. Walsh, do you sell crutches?" he asked as soon as he opened the door.

"No, but we loan them. You don't look like you need crutches."

"Not for me. The new school teacher fell and sprained her ankle. Thought she might need some crutches."

Mr. Walsh smiled at Nate. "She must be a nice young lady to inspire a man to present her with crutches."

Nate looked away, then said, "She's new in town. Just thought I'd lend a hand."

"Now, tell me, Nate, is she pretty?"

"Well, yes. She has a pretty face and auburn hair. But that's not the point."

"The point is, Nate, you're a fine young man who's going on twenty-five years of age, yet you never give the time of day to any of the young ladies around here. Maybe this is the one."

"Gotta make some money first. Now, how about those crutches?"

"How tall is she?"

"How would I know?

"I don't know, but I need to know, so I can select the right size crutches."

"Oh. In that case, I'd say the top of her head comes up to about my nose."

"Let me look in the back and see what I've got in that size."

Mr. Walsh disappeared through a curtained doorway, leaving Nate to wonder how Carrie would react if he arrived with a pair of crutches. She probably wouldn't be too pleased. The bigger question in his head was why he kept looking for ways to see Carrie again, even if it meant buying a pair of crutches. He was mighty glad Mr. Walsh would loan them because money was tight. Half his lemon orchard had died in the deep freeze of

1913 and the continuing drought. He hoped he'd have a crop this year that would at least cover expenses. Since he'd met Carrie, he wanted more than anything to be financially successful, but it didn't look likely to happen very soon.

Chapter Five

Carrie hadn't moved far from the couch in the living room most the day because every time she did, her ankle ached. At dinnertime, she hobbled slowly to and from the table, then sank once again onto the couch. Bertie came with a fresh ice pack, then brought coffee for all three of them, and they settled into an evening of reading the paper together, sharing sections of it with each other.

They looked up from their reading when they heard steps on the front porch and then a knock on the door. Mr. Owens went to the door and opened it. "Well, hello, Mr. Jenkins. I presume this is your boy with you. Please come in."

"We came to see Miss Carolyn Wyngate." Mr. Jenkins, a bulky man dressed in a dark suit, white shirt and tie stepped into the room. The boy hung back.

"She's right here." Mr. Owens waved his arm toward the couch, and Carrie pulled herself into a more upright sitting position.

"Hello, Miss Wyngate. I had intended to greet you and welcome you to the school under different circumstances."

The man's stare made Carrie feel uncomfortable. She rallied a smile. "This isn't the way I planned to meet the principal of the Chula Vista Elementary school, either."

Mr. Jenkins didn't smile back. Instead, he pushed his son toward Carrie. "This is my boy, Charlie. He'll be one of your students."

Carrie looked at the boy, whose eyes were staring at the floor. Nudged by his father, he stumbled toward her. He stood with his head down, a mop of brown curly hair flopping onto his forehead. A thin child, he was browned by a summer in the sun. Carrie guessed he was nine years old.

"Hi, Charlie. Nice to meet you." She extended her hand, and Charlie limply took it. His small hand felt sweaty in hers.

"Now Charlie, you tell Miss Wyngate what you came to say."

The boy still didn't look up, but half stuttered, "I. . .I'm sorry. . .I ran. . .into you."

Carrie kept quiet as her mind raced with this revelation. "Charlie, I didn't even see you, and I don't think you saw me, either, until the last minute. It was an accident."

"Don't make excuses for the boy, Miss Wyngate," Mr. Jenkins cut in.

Carrie looked at Charlie just as he raised his chin a little. His eyes looked like those of a trapped animal. He tried to look away, but she smiled and kept her eyes on him. "I accept your apology, Charlie. You are a very responsible boy to come here and apologize."

The boy glanced at Carrie with a tiny spark of connection in his eyes as he softly asked, "Are you hurt bad?"

"Not at all. Just a sprained ankle. Aunt Bertie's been keeping ice on it all day, and I'm going to be up walking around here before anybody knows it." Carrie shifted her eyes to Mr. Jenkins. "In fact, I should be able to make it to the school tomorrow, so you can show me my room and get me acclimated to everything."

"Don't rush things, Miss Wyngate. Stay off that ankle for a couple more days. Come into the school on Friday."

"Thank you, Mr. Jenkins. And Charlie, I'll be seeing you when school starts."

"Good evening, Miss Wyngate. Charlie, tell Miss Wyngate goodbye."

Charlie stared at the ground again. "Goodbye, Miss Wyngate."

Mr. Owens ushered Mr. Jenkins and his son out the front door, returned to his overstuffed chair and picked up the newspaper again. As he sat down, he said, "Now we know the rest of the story."

"Yes," Carrie said. "I felt sorry for that little boy. I don't think he intended any harm to me. He just got scared and ran."

"Looked like he was still scared this evening," Bertie added.

Carrie stopped herself from saying what she was thinking. Though she didn't fault the father for requiring the boy to confront his wrongs and apologize to her, she felt the man was intimidating. A sense of dread settled over her. How could she possibly work with this man all year? He was not what she had hoped for in a principal. How complicating to have his son as one of her students. She hoped she could help the boy in some way without irritating the father.

Ten minutes later, her thoughts were interrupted by another knock on the door. Mr. Owens moved toward it and opened it. "Good evening, Nate. Come in. What brings you around?"

Nate stepped in, and when she saw him, she caught her breath. He was carrying a set of crutches. At that moment, his eyes met hers, and she tried not to reflect the anger she felt rising inside her. Why had he appointed himself as her caretaker? She didn't need it or want it.

"Hello, Carrie," he said as he walked toward her.

Trying to keep emotion out of her voice she replied flatly, "Hello, Nate."

"I got to thinking today that a pair of crutches might help you get around while the ankle is healing."

"How thoughtful!" Bertie interjected before Carrie could say a word.

Carrie quickly found her voice and her manners. "Thank you, Nate."

"Where did you find crutches in this town?" Mr. Owens asked.

"The drugstore. It was a hunch I had, which paid off. Mr. Walsh keeps several on hand of different sizes to loan out to people as needed."

Mr. Owens looked at Carrie. "Are you ready to try them to see if they fit?"

"I guess so," Carrie replied as she moved her legs to the side of the sofa. Once again, an arrow of pain shot through her ankle.

Nate leaned the crutches against the couch and stepped toward her to give her his arm to support her as she stood. Then he reached for the crutches and handed them to Carrie, who placed one under each arm. Nate smiled. "Looks like they're the perfect fit."

"Looks that way," Bertie said. "Try taking a step or two, Carrie."

Carrie did. It felt awkward, but she had to admit that the crutches were the correct length and would probably be very helpful on her way to recovery.

"Thanks, Nate. I think this is going to work. How did you know what size?" Carrie looked at him.

"A lucky guess. Mr. Walsh is pretty good at this stuff. He said for you not to take any long walks. That means you shouldn't walk to school on crutches," Nate teased.

Bertie and her husband laughed while Carrie tried to, but she couldn't shake the irritation that Nate was monitoring her life too closely for her comfort.

A few minutes later, Nate said goodbye and left. "That was nice of him," Bertie said. She looked at her husband, who simply nodded his head but said nothing

As Archie Owens and his wife, Bertie, got ready for bed later that evening, they talked of Nate and Carrie. "He's really interested in her," Bertie observed.

Archie agreed and added that he hadn't seen Nate take interest in any of the local women before. "Maybe this will work for him. He's an awfully nice kid. Works hard. Has an interest in the community."

"But Carrie brushes him off. Maybe I ought to talk with her and tell her what an admirable young man Nate is."

"I think we should stay out of it."

"I knew you'd say that, Archie. Don't you have any interest in romance?"

"Ours, but nobody else's." He put his arm around his wife and drew her to him, kissing her on the lips. "See what a romantic I am?" he said before he kissed her again.

"Oh, Archie."

They turned off the lamp, slipped into bed and snuggled into each other's arms.

Chapter Six

Carrie didn't sleep well. Her ankle throbbed, and the thoughts in her head kept looping around and around like a carousel going in circles but never getting anywhere. She worried about how she would get along with Mr. Jenkins. She wondered if Charlie would ever trust her after their accidental beginning. She fretted about time lost while her ankle mended. In response to that, she began making mental lists of things she wanted to do to prepare for the soon-coming school year.

Finally, she puzzled over Nate Landon, reminding herself to discourage him from any further interest in her. It shouldn't be hard to do if he weren't so attractive. She pulled the blanket over her face, then threw it off, watched shadow patterns on the ceiling, forced her eyelids to close, opened them again. Eventually, she slept.

The next day, Carrie felt better and found she could walk quite well with the crutches. The thought of sitting inside the house for the entire day had no appeal. She was determined to go outside, at least to the front porch to sit and enjoy the day. Taking a book, a journal and a pen, she sat in the wicker rocker looking over the lemon orchards that stretched in every direction. It looked like an ocean of green. Here and there, rooftops punctuated the leafy waves, Victorian towers rising to the sun. The houses were evenly spread around the community, each one situated in the middle of an orchard. She wondered how much land each of the homeowners owned and marveled that people could afford to have so much space around them. In Chicago, she had always lived in an apartment in a building smack against another building. Maybe some day she would own a home surrounded by trees.

Picking up her pen, she began writing in her journal, putting the experiences of the last two days to paper. She wrote without stopping for several minutes, then lifted the pen, stared ahead and frowned. What did she want to write about Nate? She always tried to be honest about the feelings she expressed in her journal, but her feelings about Nate were like a stew of many ingredients that she was afraid to stir up.

Her thoughts were interrupted by laughter. Looking toward the sound, she saw two little girls coming down the street toward the Owenses' house. They were holding hands and skipping together but not always in sync, which is what produced the giggles. Both had long hair, though one was blonde and the other a brunette. The big bows in their hair, one yellow, one pink, bounced as they skipped.

Carrie smiled, and at that moment the brunette looked her way. The girl must have said something to her friend because both turned toward her. Carrie waved at them and they took it as an invitation to skip up the front walk. They stopped at the bottom of the stairs, panting and giggling at the same time. Then they got quiet. "Can't you walk?" the brunette asked as her eyes took in the crutches leaning against Carrie's chair.

"Yes, I can walk, but I fell and sprained my ankle yesterday, so I'm using crutches while it heals. I'll be walking, maybe even running like you girls, in a couple of days. By the way, I'm Miss Carolyn Wyngate, the new fourth-grade teacher. What are your names?"

The hand of the blonde girl flew to her mouth. "Oh, you'll be my teacher. I'm Jennie Landon."

At the sound of the last name, Carrie's mind immediately asked, "Nate's daughter? Couldn't be. The Owens would've said something if. . .Must be a niece." She tried not to show the surprise she felt but answered, "Glad to meet you, Jennie."

"My name's Sarah Walsh," the brunette announced. "I bet you got those crutches from my dad's drugstore."

"A friend got them for me," Carrie explained, marveling at the web of connections a small town creates. "I'm happy to meet you, too, Sarah. Will you be in the fourth grade?"

"No. I'm going into fifth."

"But you're still good friends even though one of you is a year older?"

Both girls nodded their heads.

"Where were you girls headed when you came skipping down the street?"

"Nowhere."

"I see. You're just out enjoying the day like I was doing here on the front porch. Wish I could run and skip like you do."

"Do you like to jump rope, Miss. . .Miss. . . . "

"Wyngate."

"Miss Wyngate."

"Love it. At least I used to. I got pretty good at double Dutch."

Both girls squealed. "We jump double Dutch at school all the time," Jennie said. "I can't wait for school to start."

"Me, too," Sarah echoed.

"What are your favorite subjects?"

"I love reading," Jennie said as she hopped from one foot to the other.

"Reading's okay, but I like math best." Sarah bumped her hip against Jennie, which set them both giggling.

At that moment, the front door opened, and Mrs. Owens walked out. "I heard all the fun out here and didn't want to miss anything." She smiled. "How are you girls today?"

"Fine."

"Would you like to have some cookies and lemonade?"

Jennie and Sarah nodded their heads, and Carrie said, "Sounds lovely."

Bertie returned inside the house and came back minutes later with a plate of sugar cookies, a pitcher of lemonade and four glasses on a silver tray. She set it on a small table and invited everyone to the treats.

Jennie and Sarah drank their lemonade and ate their cookies while sitting on the top step of the porch. Bertie served Carrie, then pulled a wicker chair next to hers and sat down. "Such a lovely morning," she said as she lifted a glass of lemonade to her mouth.

Ten minutes later, Sarah said, "We'd better go pretty soon, Jennie. Our mothers'll be worried."

Both girls stood up, faced Bertie and said thank you for the refreshments. Immediately, they turned around, linked arms and skipped down the pathway to the street.

"Oh, to be young again," Bertie said. "They're such cute girls."

"They are. Did you know Jennie will be one of my students this year?"

"Is she in fourth grade already?"

"Guess so. She said her name was Jennie Landon. Is she Nate's— "

"Niece. His older brother's daughter."

"Sarah said her father owns the drugstore where the crutches came from. Everybody in this town must be related or have some connection to some one else."

"That's the nice thing about small towns." Bertie set her empty glass back on the tray. "And the bad thing about small towns." She laughed.

Carrie laughed too. "Guess I'll have to watch my words around here." In her mind, she didn't laugh but seriously wondered how she would fare in this community. I'll have to listen a lot more than I talk, she told herself, something she had already started practicing back in Chicago.

Bertie stood, gathered up the tray and headed into the house. Carrie followed, hopping with the help of the crutches. "Is there something I can do to help you, Bertie? I'm really getting bored sitting around."

"I bet you are, but you sit tight for another day. Maybe tomorrow."

It felt like tomorrow would never come, but when it did, Carrie found she could put a little weight on her ankle, making it possible to hop around the house without crutches. She wanted to get outside but confined herself to the front porch, where she could watch people coming and going. The street was nothing like the streets of Chicago. The avenue she had lived on was always crowded with people, automobiles and horse-drawn buggies all vying for a place. Here, in Chula Vista, she counted no more than half a dozen folk walking and only two automobiles during the entire afternoon.

She mostly liked the quieter pace, but when she realized how far she was in time and space from her childhood, she felt sad. It had been a short time since her grandmother died, yet it felt like she'd been without her forever. Other times, it felt she'd lost her yesterday. As for her parents, she didn't let herself think about them too much, else the years of loss would pile up on her and nearly crush her spirit. She simply touched the locket hanging from her neck and tried to think of happier things.

This was the somber mood she was in when Mr. Owens walked up the driveway. "Hello, there!" he said as he came up the steps toward her. "Had a nice day?"

"Very nice. The air is so clear and warm, actually hot, except it's nice here in the shade. When does fall weather come?"

Archie Owen sat down in a nearby chair and chuckled. "If you're talking about leaves changing color, frost on the pumpkin and all that, the answer is hardly ever. Except for the freeze two years ago, it hardly ever dips below forty degrees around here. By November or December, leaves on some of the trees in people's yards turn gold or red."

"It never snows?"

"No. Occasionally the mountains receive a dusting of snow."

"Can't imagine what it's going to be like to live in a place without winter as I've always known it."

"It's different, but you'll get used to it and enjoy it. The weather is what draws people here. I'm sure this will be quite a city one day."

Carrie tried to imagine the dirt road in front of the Owenses' house paved, cars driving back and forth on it and houses lining the street on either side. It was a picture that refused to materialize in her mind.

Archie stood. "Guess we ought to go in. Bertie'll have dinner on the table soon." He opened the front door and held it until Carrie got on her feet and hobbled into the house.

Carrie retired early that evening, promising herself that tomorrow she would walk as far as possible in the direction of the school. It would be Friday. There was only one more week until school started and she wanted to see the classroom that would be hers for the next nine months. This was the beginning of her new life, and she didn't know which excited her most—starting the new or leaving the old.

Chapter Seven

Carrie awoke the next morning with the sun again shining through her window. She loved how sunbeams slid across the floor to her bed, then climbed up onto the quilt, making the colors more vivid. Stretching, she swung her legs out of bed and stood. Her ankle felt stiff but not painful. She took a few steps. Still, no pain. Rejoicing in this evidence of healing, she reaffirmed her vow to walk to the school.

Bertie strongly urged her to stay home, but when Carrie promised to turn around and come back if her ankle hurt, the older woman conceded. At nine o'clock, Carrie started out but only covered two blocks when her ankle felt tired. There were no places to sit, so she leaned against a tree. A small figure on the opposite side of the street was heading her way. As the person grew closer, she recognized her as Jennie Landon, the girl she'd met yesterday.

Jennie looked her direction and shouted "Hi! Miss Wyngate!" Then she ran across the street asking, "Is your foot better?"

"I thought it was. I walked this far, but now I'm feeling a little tired, so I'm resting."

"Where are you going?"

"To the school. I want to see what the fourth-grade classroom looks like."

Jennie's eyes sparkled. "Oh, it's nice. It'll be fun to go to a brand new school."

"I think so, too, that's why I want to see it as soon as possible."

"I'd walk with you, but I've just come from Sarah's house, and now I've got to go to the grocery store and buy some sugar. Mom is baking and she needs it." Jennie wiggled one toe in the dirt.

"Thank you, Jennie, for the offer, but I'll be fine after I rest a few minutes. You run on home so your mother can finish her baking."

As Jennie walked away, she looked over her shoulder and said, "Bye,

Miss Wyngate."

Carrie smiled and realized how much she enjoyed children. Though she'd taught only two years, a new school year always excited her. It always had, even when she was a child. The smell of new books and freshly sharpened pencils made her happy. The scent of chalk dust and the sight of a clean blackboard waiting to receive written words, were other joys. There was never any doubt in Carrie's mind that she would be a teacher. She loved everything about it, especially the children: eager faces looking up at her, eyes that glowed at learning new concepts. It made her heart sing. Even difficult students brought her satisfaction. They challenged her to try harder and do better herself.

Adults were another matter, particularly people like Mr. Jenkins. Shuddering at the thought of him, she surmised that he did not hold the same values about children as she. Ultimately, they would clash even though she would do all in her power not to.

A man with a sack over his shoulder approached. "Good morning, Miss!"

"Good morning," she answered as she wondered what he was carrying. It looked awfully heavy and bulky. "You've got quite a load."

"Bag of chicken feed." He set it down at his feet and faced her. "Name's Woodson." "Hello, Mr. Woodson. I'm Carolyn Wyngate, the new fourth-grade teacher."

"Welcome to Chula Vista. You're lucky to be one of the first ones to teach in our new school. We're mighty proud of it. I'm one of the carpenters who worked on it."

"It looks like a well-made building. I've only seen the outside, but was walking down there so I could go inside and inspect my new quarters."

Mr. Woodson lifted the bag of chicken feed back to his shoulder. "Hope you like it. There's some folks in town don't. They think it cost too much. Mr. Owens is one of 'em. Every time I went into his barbershop to get a haircut, he picked and fussed about every penny spent on the school."

Carrie looked Mr. Woodson in the eyes and said, "I'm sure I'll like the new school. Thanks for your part in constructing it."

He smiled at her compliment. "Gotta get going. The chickens are hungry. Good day, Miss Wyngate."

"Good day to you," she said as she lifted her hand in a wave. As he walked away, his comment about Mr. Owens stuck in her head like a burr, until she picked it off and discarded it with the thought that nobody is perfect. These first few days in Chula Vista reminded her of starting a puzzle. There are lots of pieces lying around. You keep picking up random ones and look for a place they fit. Slowly, a picture takes shape. Carrie considered it might be a long time before an accurate picture of this community and her place in it might emerge; meanwhile, she would do what she came to do—teach children. The piece of the puzzle that she wanted most to put in place today was to see the school house. She put her good foot forward, then the other. It felt weak and wobbly. How much farther was it to the school? Another block or two? She'd walked at least two blocks to get this far. Her head told her she should go home. Her heart urged her forward. Halfway across an uneven street, her mind told her she wouldn't want to stub her toe on anything and possibly fall again, so she turned around.

Returning to the Owenses' front porch, she sank into a chair, hot and sweaty and unhappy that she'd failed to reach her goal for the day. Bertie fussed over her, bringing another ice pack, making sure her leg was propped up.

It was over Saturday night dinner that Mr. Owens invited Carrie to attend church with them on Sunday morning. "It's a great place to make new friends," he said. "We have a lot of young people in the congregation. I think you'd enjoy it."

"What church is it?" she asked, not that it mattered much since she hadn't attended any church for many months.

"Community Congregational." Mr. Owens said as he spooned mashed potatoes onto his plate. "It's the first church to be built in our city. It's on F Street near the center of town."

Carrie looked up from buttering a slice of bread. "Is that the church next to the old school where I fell?"

Mr. Owens nodded.

"Since I've been laid up with this ankle, it'll be good to get out. Thanks for inviting me."

The next day, walking out of church after the service, she nearly bumped into Nate, who stood on the front sidewalk as though waiting for someone. Noting how good he looked in a suit and tie, Carrie felt her resolve to discourage him crumbling. He tilted his head toward her, eyebrows pulled inward. "You're not using the crutches."

"No, but I'm keeping the ankle wrapped."

He looked at her feet and asked in a low voice. "You're doing better?"

"Yes. Thank you for your concern."

At that moment, another young man sidled up, saying, "Who's this charming young lady?"

Between tightened lips, Nate spoke in formal tones.

"Arthur, meet Miss Carolyn Wyngate. Carolyn, this is an old school chum, Arthur Stone."

The introductions had barely concluded when Arthur winked at Carrie and asked, "What brings such a beautiful woman to our town?"

"She's the new fourth-grade teacher," Nate cut in.

Arthur kept his eyes on Carrie. "Makes a man wish he could go back to being a school kid, doesn't it, Nate?"

"Excuse us, Arthur, I was about to walk Miss Wyngate home." Nate stepped closer to Carrie and extended his arm.

Taking it, Carrie looked sideways at Arthur and said, "Nice to meet you, Mr. Stone."

They stepped past Arthur and walked away without looking back at him.

"You don't need to walk me home. I'm riding with the Owens."

"Oh. . . . Well. . . . That's a good thing. You probably shouldn't be walking much."

"I suppose not, but I'm tired of being unable to go anywhere on my own."

Nate cleared his throat. "Would you be interested in resurrecting my offer of the other day? For a tour? Get you out of the house?"

"Sounds tempting."

"I could find an older woman to come along as a chaperone."

The physical contact of her arm in his weighted Carrie's decision to the positive. "I accept."

"Good. I'll pick you up about three this afternoon."

"Fine. And since this is a professional tour, I don't think we need a chaperone."

"You're sure?" Nate asked.

"Positive."

Chapter Eight

Entering her room at the Owenses' house, Carrie sat on the edge of the bed, pulled off her shoes and unwrapped the injured ankle. As she rubbed it, she thought about her comment to Nate about not needing a chaperone.

You don't know what the rules for teachers might be in Chula Vista.

True. But the school year has not begun. Besides, it's only small, rural schools that hang onto outdated laws against socializing. There weren't any such restrictions in Chicago.

This isn't Chicago.

I'm twenty-two. Old enough to handle my own life.

She tossed her shoe across the room, stood and walked to the small closet, opening it to study what to wear later that afternoon. Choosing a light green summer frock, a large-brimmed white hat and a pair of white gloves, she laid them across the bed and hurried downstairs to the Sunday lunch Bertie had prepared.

Mr. Owens sat at the table discussing the opinion piece he'd read in the Sunday morning paper. "The writer thinks we'll soon be in this war in Europe."

"I hope not!" Bertie said as she set a platter of fried chicken on the table. "We have no business sticking our noses into other people's fights."

"Don't forget the sinking of the Lusitania last May. 128 Americans died in that attack by the Germans."

Carrie pulled out a chair at the side of the table and sat down. Archie looked her direction.

"What do you think about the war in Europe?"

"I think any war is awful. I'd hate to see our country get involved." Carrie unfolded the napkin beside her plate and spread it in her lap.

"Even though it was a direct attack by an enemy on our people and the English?"

Bertie placed her hand on her husband's shoulder. "Please, Archie. Let's leave off the war talk and have a peaceful Sunday lunch."

"Of course, Bertie." Archie stood, pulled out a chair and seated his wife at the table.

After lunch and kitchen clean-up, Carrie dressed in the clothes she had laid across her bed earlier, replacing the white ribbon on her hat with a green tulle one which she tied into a bow in the back. Picking up a small fabric handbag, she headed downstairs and out to the front porch to wait for Nate.

A few minutes later, he drove up, parked, walked briskly up the front path and took two of the porch steps at a time until he stood before her. He wore black, cuffed slacks and a white shirt but no tie. With arm out, palm up, he bowed. "At your service, Miss, for the grand tour of Chula Vista."

She smiled, took his hand and stood.

He escorted her down the steps and toward his truck. "You can sit for the entire trip. Never take a single step."

Opening the car door, he helped her in and started whistling as he trotted around to the driver's seat. In minutes they were rolling down F Street. When they reached Third Avenue, he turned right and pointed toward Shafer's Hardware. "That's where I saw US Army troops four years ago."

"What was the Army doing here?"

"Mexican Revolution. Battle of Tijuana. We didn't want the revolution coming here. We're not far from the border, you know."

"How far?"

"Eight miles."

They had barely passed the hardware store when Nate pointed left. "That building over there is a lemon packing plant. There are several more in the area. My older brother, James, is the manager for one of them."

Carrie looked in the direction Nate pointed. "In Chicago I saw boxes of lemons and oranges stamped with California labels. I never dreamed I'd be here one day."

"I'm glad you are." Nate looked her way, but she didn't look at him.

He continued in his tour-guide voice. "That particular packing plant has a fruit washer operated by an electric motor. The man who invented the machine built the Owenses' house."

"You mean I live on a piece of Chula Vista history?

Nate chuckled, but kept his eyes on the dirt street ahead of him. A few more blocks down the road, he pointed out another building on a corner. That's where the Japanese farm workers gather to wait for someone to hire them in the orchards."

"Do you hire Japanese workers?"

"No. We're really a very small orchard and so far have been able to get along with family help, plus a couple of Mexicans."

A hot breeze blew across Carrie's face. She dug in her handbag, pulled out a fan, opened it and started fanning herself. "Where do they live?"

"Where does who live?"

"The Japanese. I haven't seen any, but of course I haven't been here long."

"Many of them have farms south and east of here in the Otay River Valley. Others are in the Sweetwater valley. A few live in town."

Nate turned west at the next corner, and soon they were driving along the bay. Sunlight sparkled on the water. "Right up ahead is the Western Salt Company. Established in 1902."

Carrie peered ahead to see what looked like rectangular squares of white at the edge of the bay.

"That's where they let sun evaporate water until they have salt."

Nate made a U-turn in the road and pointed across the bay. "That strip of land is what they call the Silver Strand. On the other side is the Pacific Ocean. Farther up there in the distance is the famous del Coronado hotel. You can't see it from here. It's got a red, cone-shaped roof."

Carrie squinted.

"You can get there by the electric train or go into downtown San Diego and take the ferry. Perhaps we can do that sometime. The hotel is so fancy. Huge dining and dance rooms with windows that look out on the ocean."

"Sounds beautiful," is all Carrie said. Nate's assumption that he could take her there sometime made her uneasy. This was supposed to be a therapeutic drive, not the launching of a relationship. She swished the fan vigorously in front of her face, as if cooling her skin might untangle her thoughts about the young man beside her.

They drove along in silence for several minutes, Nate's left arm half-in, half-out of the window, his other hand on the steering wheel. "It's so beautiful here," he said softly.

Carrie looked at him quickly, then away. It was nice that he cared about his hometown.

"It was a great place to grow up," he continued. "I used to go fishing off that pier up ahead of us. That's a dock for the San Diego Yacht Club." He glanced her way. "Did you ever go fishing, Carrie?"

"No. I never had any friends or family members who were fishermen. I guess a lot of people fished in Lake Michigan, but not me."

"Then I'll have to take you."

Carrie grimaced, wishing that Nate would stop putting the two of them together in his plans. He was a likable person. Optimistic. Enthusiastic. Good looking. It was hard to dislike him, but she had made promises to herself that she intended to keep.

Nate turned east on E Street. "Let's drive a little ways up the Sweetwater Valley."

"Will I see some Japanese farms?

"Maybe. Why are you so interested in Japanese people?"

"Because I never met any Asian people. Most the immigrants in Chicago were from northern Europe. Or Italy."

Nate chuckled. "Maybe we can stir some up for you." Then he turned somber. "Actually, the Japanese are the ones stirring things up around here."

"What do you mean by that?"

"There are tensions between us and them."

"What about?"

"Land. Give them an inch and who knows how much they'll take."

Carrie's hand flew to her mouth to hide a gasp of surprise. "Are they stealing property?"

"No. Yes. Sort of. We just passed a Land Act here in California in 1913 to keep them from stealing our land."

Carrie tried to keep her voice calm. "What is this Land Act?"

"You must be a citizen to own property."

"Sounds reasonable. Surely some of the Japanese have been here long enough to be citizens. Or their children would be natural-born citizens."

"Except federal law excludes Asians from becoming citizens."

"Really!" Carrie gasped. "I didn't know that, and I don't like it."

"Check it out for yourself, Carrie. The Japanese have been very clever in getting around the law. They buy or rent land in their children's names. Or find some soft-hearted person who will rent to them. We've got to put a stop to this." Nate's voice rose like a soap-box preacher warming up to a hell-and-damnation sermon.

Carrie sat still, not daring to look at Nate, not seeing any of the scenery as they continued driving. Nate's opinions shocked her. She felt displeasure rising in her, threatening to turn to combativeness. She wanted to argue the issue but felt ill informed, so she clamped her mouth shut and decided to investigate the issue of the Japanese in Chula Vista and the laws of California making it impossible for them to own land. She would read and inform herself so she could speak well the next time the topic came up. And she was sure it would.

Nate looked toward her. "You don't agree with me. I can feel it."

"I don't know enough about the issue, so I'll not argue with you; but off-hand, I don't agree with you."

Nate kept driving, his eyes pin-pointed on the dirt road ahead. Finally, he said, "Let's just drop it. Sorry I got a bit heated up. You're new here. You don't see the whole picture, but you will." He glanced briefly at Carrie. "Well, wouldn't you know it, there's a Japanese farm on the right. The whole family's out working in their fields. That's another thing about them. They don't take Sundays off. Work all the time. Creates an unfair advantage for them over the rest of us."

Carrie half heard Nate's last few words. She was looking at two adults, dressed in what looked like billowy pants with a long tunic worn on the top. They were bent over a row of some kind of plants. Next to them were two children doing the same, except the children looked up as she and Nate drove past.

Carrie smiled and waved at them. They waved back, and she thought she saw them smile. It made her feel good. "Do they speak English?"

"Not the older people. That's another problem in doing business with them. They don't speak English. We don't speak Japanese. The children learn to speak English, though. Maybe you'll be lucky to have one or two in your classroom."

Carrie chose to ignore the sarcasm in Nate's voice. "I'd love to help children like that learn."

As they drove on, they talked of other things, inconsequential topics that might reduce the tension that had risen between them. An hour later, Nate parked in front of the Owenses' home, helped Carrie out of the car and delivered her to the front door.

"Thank you, Nate, for the tour. You really know a lot about your town."

"You're welcome, Carrie. I've always believed people should appreciate and do what they can for their community." He looked earnestly into her eyes.

"You're doing a good job of that," she said as she placed her hand on the doorknob.

He gave her a half-smile, said goodbye and walked back to his truck. Carrie noticed that he did not whistle. The afternoon had not gone well, and she tried to feel fine with it. After all, she had wanted to discourage him, and she guessed that their difference of opinion had successfully done that.

As Carrie slowly climbed the stairs to her room, she was surprised at the sadness she felt.

Chapter Nine

The next week passed quickly. Carrie walked to the school on Monday and inspected the fine, new building. There were eight large classrooms with big windows. Her room was the first down the hall to the right. Mr. Jenkins had been cordial and introduced her to all the other teachers, each one busy setting up their individual rooms.

Carrie felt especially drawn to the first-grade teacher, a young woman named Mary Snyder, who bubbled with life. "Let's eat our lunches together," she invited.

Standing in the middle of her classroom, Carrie faced the window that looked out onto F Street. She liked the light it brought in. Her eyes surveyed the room. There were four rows of five desks each, but when she picked up the roster on her desk, it contained only a dozen names. More students would probably sign up during the week and on the first day of school. She sat down at the teacher's desk at the center front of the room, read the names and felt a thrill of excitement about meeting these students. Taking up a pen, she jotted down plans for the first day, especially the opening moments when she would introduce herself and take roll call. Checking the list to see if there were any names that might be difficult to pronounce, she came upon "David Imamura." It fascinated her that his name reflected his dual roots, and she wondered how well adjusted the boy might be to an American school. How well could he speak, write and read English? That would be her task—to give this child of two worlds a solid foundation in the three Rs and shape him into an American citizen. What a wonderful job I have.

There was a stack of McGuffie Readers and arithmetic books piled on the desk, waiting dispersal to each pupil. Inside the drawer were two boxes of fresh chalk, and new erasers were on the tray of the blackboard, She had to write a class schedule on the board but first needed to figure it out. Picking up a pen and sheet of paper, she began jotting down items.

9 a.m.—Welcome—Pledge of Allegiance to the flag—Prayer

9:15 a.m.—Arithmetic Instruction

9:30 to 9:45—Arithmetic Practice

It took her the rest of the morning to finalize the schedule on paper. Then, she took up a piece of chalk and wrote the schedule on the left side of the board, using her best penmanship. Children learn by example, she believed.

"Ready for lunch?" Mary poked her head in the door. "Let's sit outside."

"Be right there." Carrie stacked the loose papers on her desk, put pen and pencils in the drawer and picked up her lunch basket.

The two young women walked down the hall and out the back door of the school, where they sat on the edge of the porch overlooking the play yard. It didn't amount to much: a huge square of dirt, a swing set and two teeter-totters set on the edge of it. The lack of grass made it look like a desert. Carrie wondered how mothers felt about their children playing in the dirt in their school clothes. When she reflected on it, she realized there wasn't much grass anywhere in Chula Vista and she attributed that to the arid climate and the ongoing drought everybody was concerned about.

Mary opened her lunch basket, retrieved a sandwich wrapped in wax paper and set it on her lap. "Is this your first year of teaching?"

"No. I've taught two years. What about you?" Carrie pulled a sandwich out of her basket and unwrapped it.

"This'll be my third year. I love it."

Carrie bit into the sandwich and asked, "Have you always taught first grade?"

"My first year of teaching was in a one-room country school, where I taught all grades."

"That must've been challenging. I never had a multiple-grade classroom."

"It keeps you busy. It's nice having only one grade."

The two young women chatted about their teaching experiences until Mary stopped and looked at Carrie. "I never asked where you came from."

"I'm from Chicago."

"Whew! That's a long way from here. How'd you get here?"

"On the train." Carrie grinned at Mary, who grinned back at her. "I wanted to get away from the big city and see the rest of the country. Then I heard of this job, applied for it and got it, so here I am. Where did you grow up?"

"San Diego. I went a long way, didn't I? Two train stops from home." Mary chuckled. "What's it like in Chicago?"

"It's pretty in the summer along the lake. Lots of trees and green lawns. Like anywhere else, there's a bad part of the city, too."

"Where the Chicago Mafia hang out?"

Carrie didn't answer, and Mary looked her way with a puzzled expression in her eyes. Carrie nodded, but still didn't say anything. Mary shrugged her shoulders and took another bite of her sandwich. Finally, Carrie found her voice. "My grandmother and I lived in an apartment....in a nice area." She choked up. Tears crept to her eyes, and she brushed them away with the handkerchief she always carried in her pocket.

"What's wrong, Carrie?"

Carrie swallowed hard. "I lost my grandmother a few months ago. It all came rushing back when I started talking about where we lived."

"I'm sorry for your loss. You must have been very close."

Carrie nodded but didn't trust herself to speak, so she and Mary sat together silently. It puzzled her that sometimes she could speak of her grandmother in a normal manner. Other times, she cried. Mary's mention of the mafia had also upset her in a way she hadn't expected. Dark fear rose from somewhere deep inside her. She thought she'd left it in Chicago. Here it was again. Like a lion, crouched, ready to spring.

Carrie took a deep breath and tried to sound casual as she asked, "What do people do around here for entertainment?"

"Have you heard of the Panama Exposition? It opened in San Diego in Balboa Park the first of this year. It's a lot of fun: exhibits, all kinds of concession stands, games, food. A group of us are going this Saturday night. Want to come? Please do. You'd love it and it would be a good way for you to meet more young people."

"I'd love to," Carrie said as she stood, facing Mary. "Right now, I need to get back in the classroom and finish up a few more things before I call it a day."

"Me too, but let me know when you're ready to go home. We can walk together."

Later that afternoon, Carrie cleared her desk, gathered up some papers and put them in her lunch basket, placed her hat on her head and closed the door to her classroom. She met Mary in the hall, and the two women walked out the front door.

"Where are you boarding?" Mary asked.

"525 F Street." Carrie pointed west. "With Mr. and Mrs. Owens."

Mary laughed. "That means this is as far as we'll be walking together because I live the opposite direction. 155 G Street."

Carrie smiled. "No. This is not as far we can walk together. We've got the whole driveway to go before we part company."

Both women laughed as they walked toward F Street and turned in opposite directions.

"Hello, Carrie!" Bertie's voice sang from the kitchen. "How did things go for you today?"

"Very well!" Carrie said as she drifted into the room where Bertie sat at the table peeling potatoes. She let herself sink into a chair, set her bag on the table and gave a contented sigh.

Bertie glanced at her. "Any trouble with the ankle?"

"Didn't even think about it till you mentioned it right now. Guess it's completely healed." Carrie leaned over and looked at her ankle, checking her statement against the evidence. "I met the nicest person today. The first grade teacher. Her name is Mary."

"Mary Snyder?"

"Yes. Do you know her?"

"Not personally, but I've heard parents say how pleased they are with her as a teacher. Other people say she's quite a socialite. Always running into the city with a group of young men and women to this and that event."

"She invited me to go with her to the Panama Exposition this Saturday night."

"Should be fun, but don't stay out as late as I've heard she does."

"What does it matter how late it is since it'll be on a Saturday night?" Immediately, Carrie knew her comment was impertinent, but Bertie shrugged her shoulders and kept peeling a potato.

"Doesn't matter at all, as long as you're able to rise on Sunday morning and attend church without being drowsy."

Carrie squirmed in her chair as she realized she did not want to attend church with Bertie and her husband every week. Churchgoing was not part of her regular routine, not since....well, not for a long time. What she couldn't admit, not even to herself, was that she was angry with God.

The week passed quickly, and Saturday afternoon arrived, another warm day with clear blue skies and a whisper of breeze blowing from the bay. Carrie put on a lavender dress, draped a shawl over her arm against the possibility of a cool evening and walked toward the train stop where she saw half a dozen people standing together. As she drew closer, she saw Mary standing in the middle of the group, talking and laughing, her brown curls bouncing against her cheeks.

"Hello, Carrie! Come meet everybody!" Mary beckoned. There were three young women, besides Mary, and three young men. As Mary introduced her to all of them, Carrie heard a familiar sound: Nate's truck. He parked across the street from them, jumped out of the vehicle and sauntered toward them. "This is Nate," Mary said, to which Nate replied. "We've already met."

He nodded toward Carrie and said, "Good evening." She responded the same, then they both stood awkwardly, like they didn't know what to do next. Mary looked directly at Nate and asked, "Everybody ready to have a good time?" He glanced briefly at Mary, then looked away.

The train pulled in, and they all boarded. A young man, who had introduced himself as Miguel, situated himself so he could be next to Carrie, while Mary moved close to Nate. As they found seats on the train, Miguel sat next to Carrie, but Nate hung back so that he did not sit next to Mary. Carrie felt relieved, but the feeling didn't last.

When they arrived at Balboa Park, Carrie marveled at the beauty of it:

wide promenades, Spanish-style buildings with arches, concession stands everywhere, hawkers selling everything from liniment to hot dogs to mangoes. Tropical bushes, trees and flowers were everywhere. A clock tower stood silhouetted against a sky streaked with orange and pink as the sun set in the west.

Miguel kept hanging close to her, while she tried to keep herself in the group, not paired off with him. That is not what Mary did. All evening, Carrie watched her friend doing her utmost to capture Nate's attention. From the corner of her eye, Carrie watched their interactions, rejoicing when Nate didn't respond to Mary other than in a formal and polite way. As the evening progressed, however, Nate looked like he was more engaged with Mary, laughing with her and bending his head to attentively listen to what she had to say. Well after midnight, the group boarded the train to return to Chula Vista. Mary sat down next to Nate and wiggled in close to him. Carrie felt miserable and barely heard what Miguel, who had moved in beside her, had to say. He talked non-stop, and an occasional nod of the head or one-word comment from her was all it took to keep him going.

When they arrived in Chula Vista, Carrie watched Nate drive away with Mary in his truck while Miguel insisted on walking her home.

By the time she fell into bed, Carrie was deeply unhappy, though she tried to convince herself she was happy that Nate had moved out of her life. Isn't that what she wanted?

Chapter Ten

School began on Monday. Last-minute enrollees meant each of the twenty desks in Carrie's classroom was filled. She introduced herself, greeted the students, and read the names of each child without mispronouncing one of them. At least no one giggled.

David Imamura turned out to be a small child with dark hair and black eyes who studied her quietly. He didn't seem to hang around any of the other children: he worked alone, diligently finishing his school work. When the children passed out of the room for recess, Carrie tried to engage him in conversation. He answered with few words, though his English was better than she expected.

Within a few days, Jennie Landon had surfaced at the top of the class, with David not far behind. Charlie Jenkins struggled to stay in his seat or keep quiet, easily distracted by anything and everything. His papers came in with misspelled words and letters transposed, the d's and b's mixed up and turned backward. Carrie found herself frequently saying, "Charlie, please sit down" or "Shhh, Charlie." He was not a rebellious or mean child, and he was quick to smile when she smiled at him, but he challenged all the prescribed methods of teaching. Carrie found herself thinking about him in the evenings, wondering how to capture his attention and help him learn. She felt sure there was a bright mind hiding behind his off-putting actions. Several times, his disruptive behavior in the classroom nearly caused her to send him to the principal, but then she'd think of the sternness of Mr. Jenkins and scratch that idea. She would find a way, somehow, to deal with this child, herself, without involving his father.

The first week of classes was so busy that Carrie and Mary didn't see much of each other until Friday afternoon when they walked out of their classrooms at the same time. They met in the hallway. "How did it go for you this week?" Mary asked.

Carrie kept her eyes faced forward and simply said, "Fine."

As they reached the front door, Mary turned toward her with a twinkle in her eyes. "Want to have some fun this weekend?"

"I don't know, Mary. I've got a lot to do."

"No more than the rest of us. Come on, Carrie, take some time off."

Carrie didn't want her new friend to think anything was amiss. After all, she had no claims on Nate. In fact, she'd wanted to discourage him, so why was she still upset by what seemed to be going on between Mary and Nate last Saturday night? She hated to admit it, but she was jealous, which meant only one thing: she had feelings for Nate she didn't want to have.

"I'll think about it, Mary."

"Don't think about it too long because I'm planning a beach party and need to know how much food to bring."

"I'll let you know tomorrow morning."

The two women reached F Street when a truck rattled past them. It was Nate.

Mary waved, but he didn't see her and did not wave back. That didn't dampen Mary's spirits, however. She turned to Carrie and said, "Isn't he a darling?"

Carrie didn't have to say anything because Mary didn't take a breath before going on about Nate. "He's so handsome. And a real gentleman, too."

In her heart, Carrie couldn't have agreed more with Mary, but she hated to hear Mary talking about Nate. She wanted to get away as fast as she could, which is what she did as soon as they parted company. When Carrie reached her house, she immediately went upstairs to her room, flung off her hat, kicked off her shoes, and fell onto her bed. Anger and sadness churned inside her, finally giving way to determination. I will not let her have him. Simultaneously, her mind asked, Why not? You don't want him. Or do you?

Carrie spent the next hour drafting a note to Mary.

Dear Miss Snyder,

Thank you for your invitation to a beach party. Unfortunately, I will have to decline your kind offer. It was gracious of you to include me in your plans. Hopefully, there will be another time when I can join you.

With kindest regards,

Miss Carolyn Wyngate

Sliding the note into an envelope, she hoped to deliver it without having to face Mary. She walked downstairs and out the front door. As she descended the front steps, she saw Charlie whizzing down the street on a bicycle.

"Charlie!"

He slowed the bicycle, turned it around and pedaled to the pathway leading to the Owenses' house. He stopped, straddling the bicycle with both legs. "Yes, Miss Wyngate?"

Carrie walked rapidly toward him. "Charlie, I was wondering if you could deliver a message for me? I'll pay you a nickel." She fished in her skirt pocket, withdrew a nickel and held it up before him.

"Oh, yes, Miss Wyngate. I'd be happy to."

"It's a letter for Miss Mary Snyder. She lives at 155 G Street. Just put it in the door, ring the bell and leave."

"You don't want me to hand it to her personally?"

"That won't be necessary, Charlie. If you want to hide behind a bush and see that she gets it that would be alright, but you don't need to talk with her."

Charlie's eyes lit up with the idea of a secret mission. She handed him the envelope in one hand and the nickel in the other.

"Thank you, Miss Wyngate. I'll do just as you say." He stuffed the nickel in his pants pocket, mounted his bicycle and sped away.

Carrie watched him and thought how lucky things had turned out. Not only had she found a messenger for her note to Mary, she had acquired some goodwill from a small boy. Her day was off to a good start.

She spent the rest of the day washing and ironing clothes. While hanging a couple of shirtwaists on the line in the backyard, she noticed how hot it was. Does it ever get cool around here? It's only eleven in the morning and I'm sweating.

When she walked into the house, it felt much cooler, and she resolved to stay in the rest of the day or sit on the front porch. By late afternoon, she was tired of sitting around and half-wished she'd accepted Mary's invitation for fun, whatever that meant. Quickly, she reminded herself that if it meant seeing Mary and Nate together again, it would be misery. As the sun moved lower in the sky, she decided to walk around the block.

She heard a car come up behind her, so she stepped closer to the edge of the road. It stopped.

"Hello, Miss Wyngate!"

Jennie's head stuck out the rear window of the car, a smile lighting up her face. There was another child in the back seat—a younger brother, no doubt—a man in the driver's seat who looked a lot like Nate and a woman beside him with dark hair holding an infant on her lap.

"Miss Wyngate, these are my parents."

Jennie's father grinned. "And we have names. I'm James, my wife, Helen, baby Joseph, and our other son, Paul, in the back seat."

"A pleasure to meet all of you."

"Nice to meet you, too," Helen said. "Jennie's been talking about you non-stop ever since school started."

"I'm glad she likes school," Carrie said.

"Oh, I love school this year, 'cause you're the best teacher I ever had."

Carrie felt embarrassed at such adulation. The girl chattered on. "Mommy, Daddy, can Miss Wyngate take a ride with us?"

"I don't know. Maybe you should ask her," James said with a slight grin on his face. He sounded so much like Nate that Carrie felt her heart flutter.

Jennie made a formal invitation, and in minutes, Carrie was seated between both children in the back seat of the car. They traveled down several streets, James driving slowly so as not to stir up too much dust from the unpaved roads. On either side of the car, lemon groves stretched in every direction. Occasionally, there would be a gap in the trees and a narrow driveway would lead to a house set back from the road.

"Next house is where Grandpa and Grandma and Uncle Nate live," Jennie chattered. Carrie's heart fluttered again, and she kept her head turned to the right in the direction Jennie pointed. A break in the green trees signaled a narrow driveway. Carrie looked and saw a white, two-story house with a porch stretched across the front. Two figures sat in rocking chairs and Jennie waved to them. "Hi, Grandpa and Grandma!" They were too far away to hear, but waved.

Nate wasn't there. Carrie's heart sank. He must be with Mary.

They were practically past the house when Carrie saw Nate's truck parked next to a barn. Her heart lifted. He didn't go. Then the sinking feeling returned. He might have gone with someone else. She didn't like that idea at all so clung to the thought that he had not gone with Mary and her group of friends.

"Take Miss Wyngate past our house, too, Daddy." Jennie bounced on the seat. "It's just a little ways up here, Miss Wyngate. I want you to see where we live."

"I'd like that very much, Jennie."

They drove a few more minutes through more citrus orchards, close enough that Carrie could see the green fruit hanging on the branches. "When do the lemons get ripe?"

"May or June," James said as he turned his face toward the back seat. "Oranges are ripe in January."

"Oh. They're nice-looking trees. They remind me of a child's drawing of a tree: round, and a nice shade of green."

"You probably see a lot of children's drawings," Helen said.

"Quite a few, and I love them all. Children are such uninhibited artists."

"That's a nice way of explaining the purple clouds and pink people they color," James laughed.

"There it is!" Jennie squealed. "Our house. Right up that driveway."

Carrie looked and saw a small, one-story structure.

James had one hand on the steering wheel and the other draped over his wife's shoulder. "I don't know if you know how buying land here works, Miss Wyngate."

"No. Tell me."

"In the beginning of Chula Vista history, the San Diego Land and Trust Company sold five-acre plots for $2,000 on the condition the buyer put a house on it within six months. When we first got married, we had only enough money for the land and a very small house."

"The plan was for us to add onto the house," Helen said, "but, as you can see, it hasn't happened yet. We've added three children but no extra space."

James patted his wife's shoulder and they smiled at each other.

Half an hour later, the Landon family returned Carrie to her house on F Street. They said goodbye to each other, and Carrie walked in the house feeling contented with her day. The only thing that nagged at her mind was where Nate might have been.

Chapter Eleven

Nate had spent the day working in the orchard, clearing leaves and debris out of irrigation ditches. The soil was dry. It was time to irrigate again, but he worried about how long the water in the well and in the reservoir behind Sweetwater Dam would last. The prolonged drought was sucking the life out of everything. Tomorrow, he would turn the water on in his orchard, being careful not to waste a drop of it.

As he walked back towards the house, his mind churned with a galaxy of perplexities. The hot weather that threatened their existence. The invitation from Mary which he had declined on the basis of farm work. Carrie, a woman who captured his attention from the first moment he met her.

Mary was a nice girl and fun to be around. Quite available, too. The one thing that troubled him about Carrie was that she shut him out before he'd begun to get close. Better go with Mary, he concluded, as he kicked a clod of dirt. But I don't want to.

Nate tromped onto the back porch, sat down on a chair and yanked his dusty work shoes off, slamming them against the wall. In stockinged feet, he entered the kitchen, passed through the living room and out the front door to join his parents on the porch. He sighed as he sat down in a rocking chair.

"Tired?" his mother inquired.

Keeping his real frustrations to himself, he said, "I guess it's the heat making me tired."

"Son, you don't have to do all the work in the orchard by yourself. I can help."

"Dad, you know our agreement. I'll take care of your orchard, as well as mine, in exchange for living here with you and Mom. Besides, your health hasn't been good."

"Humph! My health. Everybody's worried about my health. Can't we forget about my health and let me enjoy life as long as I've got it?"

"Sure, Dad." Nate didn't feel like going over the argument with his dad that they'd had a hundred times. The doctor said his dad's heart wasn't as good as it should be and he ought to take it easy. Nate's father didn't know how to take it easy.

"James and the family drove by a while ago," Nate's mother said. "They had someone with them, but I couldn't see who it was." Before Nate or his father could reply, she added, "Jennie is excited about her new school teacher. Couldn't stop talking about her when she was here Friday afternoon."

Nate didn't look at his mother, though he knew she was watching for his reaction. "That's good; but then, Jennie always liked school."

They sat in silence as the shadows grew longer and the sun set behind the lemon orchard on the west side of the house. Half an hour later, Mr. Landon stood and stretched. "Come on, Agnes, let's go to bed. I've had a hard day of taking it easy."

Nate laughed as his father walked into the house. Seconds later, his mother followed, leaving Nate sitting alone in the darkness. It was too early to go to bed. Perhaps he should have gone with Mary and the group to the beach.

The alarm clock jangled him awake at five the next morning. He got out of bed immediately, dressed and trudged to the orchard to turn on the irrigation water. As the water began trickling into the ditches and eventually filling the basins around each lemon tree, Nate would keep a close watch to make sure none of the water escaped its prescribed course. He'd be in and out of the house for the next three or four hours, checking and re-checking. He should be finished in time to go to church.

There were no breaks in the ditches, and he finished in plenty of time to eat breakfast, change clothes and drive his parents to church. As the three of them entered the sanctuary, Nate saw Mary sitting on the back row, her head turned his direction, a big smile on her face. He nodded and followed his parents up the aisle to a pew on the left near the front where they always sat. A few minutes later, he saw Mr. and Mrs. Owens take their seats near the front on the right side. Carrie was not with them. Not that she had to be. She was their boarder and certainly not beholden to their comings and goings. Still, Nate couldn't help but remember that she had come with them the week before. Maybe she came by herself today. Perhaps she's sitting somewhere behind me. Though he doubted it. The only thing he was positive about was that Mary was sitting back there and she would come up to him after the services.

He felt trapped, then confused with himself for his feelings.

After the service, he deliberately kept close to his parents, but that didn't deter Mary. She came up to him, smiling and saying hello and talking about what a great time they'd had at the beach last night and it's too bad he wasn't there but she knew how important it was for him to irrigate the orchard what with this interminable heat.

Nate tried to listen attentively while looking for an opportunity to politely leave. His mother leaned into the conversation. "So good to see you, Mary. How was the first week of school?"

That took Mary onto another topic of conversation that lasted until they reached the Landons' truck. Nate held the door open while his father helped his mother in, turned to Mary, nodded and said, "Goodbye, Mary." He looked up in time to see a sly grin plastered across his father's face.

Sunday afternoon dragged. Nate tried reading a book but couldn't keep his mind on it. His parents fell asleep in their chairs on the veranda. He strolled out to the barn and poked around in the cabinet where he kept his carving tools. A half-finished duck decoy sat on the top shelf. He picked it up and studied it but set it back. Usually, that's all it would take to set him to carving for a couple of hours. Not today. He closed the cabinet and walked out of the barn.

Suddenly, he decided to drive to the bay. Minutes later, he was motoring down E Street, coming up on the intersection of Del Mar; and there stood Mary on the corner. She waved and Nate pulled up beside her. On a sudden impulse he asked, "Would you like to take a ride with me?" Immediately, he wished he hadn't.

Mary readily agreed, and Nate got out and opened the passenger door for her. She slid in, smoothing her gray skirt and adjusting her hat so it sat on her head at an angle that made her look saucy.

"Got any particular destination in mind?" she asked.

"Thought I'd go sit on the yacht club pier and dangle my feet in the water."

Mary laughed. "Sounds like a great idea for a hot day."

They must have sat together for an hour sharing life stories. Mary was easy to talk with. He told of the long trip by train that his family made when they moved from Kansas to Chula Vista fifteen years earlier. She explained what it was like to grow up in a house on a hill overlooking San Diego bay. Chula Vista was the farthest she'd ever traveled.

Finally, Nate stood and said, "It's been nice visiting with you, Mary, but I should probably take you home now." He gave her his hand to help her up. She kept hanging onto his hand as they walked back to his truck. When he got her home, she did the same thing when he helped her out of the truck. He walked her to the door and she tipped her head up toward him.

"Good evening, Mary. It's been a pleasant afternoon."

She looked disappointed. "Thank you, Nate, for the invitation."

He drove home feeling confused and frustrated.

Chapter Twelve

Within a couple of weeks, Carrie and her pupils had settled into a comfortable relationship. Every day excited her, and she reveled in each achievement the students made. Even Charlie seemed to be making progress. He calmed somewhat and kept his attention on his schoolwork for longer periods of time.

Then, one morning he came to school clearly upset by something, but instead of exhibiting uncontrolled behavior, he sat at his desk with his head down. Carrie went out of her way to engage him in speaking with her, but he turned his face from her and grunted answers to her questions.

At one point, he turned his head even more sharply than before but not before Carrie glimpsed a small purplish spot on his cheek. "It looks like you have a bruise, Charlie."

He dropped his head and mumbled, "It's nothing."

Uneasiness gripped Carrie, but she said nothing more to the boy, deciding to simply keep an eye on him. He was silent and glum all day, making little attempt to do his schoolwork.

After a few days, Charlie returned to his normal self, and Carrie told herself she had reacted too strongly to a minor observation. Two weeks later, the pattern repeated itself. Charlie was withdrawn and unresponsive. Without his knowledge, Carrie looked him over as carefully as possible but saw no physical marks of any kind. Though she could see nothing, he moved awkwardly, sitting down and getting up like his legs were stiff. What was wrong with the boy? She wished she could discuss the matter with someone.

That afternoon after school, Carrie walked to the general store before going home. As she reached the door, Nate walked out, nearly running into her.

"Pardon me. I didn't mean to—"

"It's my fault. I wasn't paying attention to where I was going."

"Something on your mind, Carrie?" Nate's voice sounded hard.

Carrie stepped back. "Would it matter to you?" As soon as the words were out of her mouth, she wanted to take them back.

"As a matter of fact, it would."

She tried not to look surprised and studied his eyes for meaning to what he'd just said. His eyes were unreadable, and he was already moving past her.

"Wait." She put out her arm, then dropped it.

"Wait for what? For you to have a heart?"

Carrie's back stiffened. Breath stuck in her throat. Ducking her head sidewise so the hat brim would partially conceal her face, she blinked rapidly and scrunched her fingers against her palms. Taking a deep breath, she forced herself to say, "Sorry. I didn't intend things to go like this."

He did not respond, and she picked another route out of the confrontation.

"You asked me a minute ago if I had something on my mind. Well, I do. It's about Charlie, the principal's boy. You remember him?" She looked at him hoping to see his eyes soften.

Nate looked away. "Of course I remember him. How long will it take for you to tell me about Charlie?"

"Not long." Carrie looked about her. "But we can't talk here."

"We could sit in my truck. It's right over there." Nate's voice still sounded hard.

Minutes later, she shared her concerns about Charlie.

"You think he's being mistreated?"

"I do. His behavior. That bruise on his cheek. The stiff way he walked."

"You have to have more evidence than that."

"I know, but I don't know how to get it and scared if I do. It could cost me my job."

"I don't know what to say." Nate shrugged his shoulders. "Except what my mother always says. 'Pray about it.'"

Carrie's voice dropped to a whisper. "I was hoping for something more helpful."

"Sorry. That's all I have to offer."

"Thank you." She reached for the door handle and Nate immediately jumped out of the truck and around to her side to open the door for her. He acts like a gentleman even when he's riled, Carrie thought as she stepped out of the truck. She glanced up and saw Mary across the street looking her way. Quickly, Mary darted into the store.

Chapter Thirteen

One Saturday morning in October, Mr. and Mrs. Owens invited Carrie to join them on a drive. "We're going to the Little Landers community today," Bertie said, "and would like you to come along so you can see more of our countryside."

"Little Landers?" Carrie raised her eyebrows. "That's a funny name for a place. I'd like to go with you just to see what it's all about."

"Good. I'll pack a picnic lunch and we'll make a day of it." Bertie opened cupboard doors and placed food items on the kitchen counter. Carrie helped, and in a short while, they had a basket jammed with bread, cold cuts, slices of cheese, raw vegetables, apples and almonds. Bertie also filled a large canteen with water.

Mr. Owens carried everything to the car and stowed it away. At the last minute, Bertie grabbed a couple of old blankets and tossed them in, too. Minutes later, they drove away in the car with all the windows down so the fresh air could wash over their faces.

"Archie, tell Carrie about Little Landers," Bertie said as she pushed her hat more firmly on her head.

Archie turned his head halfway toward the back seat, where Carrie sat. "Little Landers is an experiment by a magazine editor in San Francisco and a horticulturist in San Diego. Their idea was that a person could provide for his family by growing most his own food. On a piece of ground as little as an acre. That's how the name Little Landers came about."

Carrie leaned forward. "That's interesting. How is the concept working?"

"Fairly well, I guess. At least there are several nice farms in the bottom lands of the river and on the adjoining hillsides. The founders laid out a model town site with streets, a park and locations for a school, clubhouse and civic center."

"So it's a town made up of little farms," Carrie said.

"Originally, a person could buy an acre, a half acre, or even just a quarter of an acre. The smaller portions are about all one person can handle."

"I imagine so. Are most of the people farmers?"

"People from all walks of life from all over the country settled in the area: teachers, lawyers, doctors, artists, bankers, mechanics. Actually, there were only a few experienced farmers. They all help each other. Kind of a communal thing."

Bertie twisted her body so she could face Carrie. "They grow everything. Peaches, apricots, figs, berries, oranges—lemons, of course—but also guavas and tropical fruits. Almonds, olives. All sorts of vegetables: tomatoes, corn, celery, spinach. They sell a lot of produce at farmer's markets."

"It sounds like a paradise," Carrie said as she looked out the car window.

They traveled south from Chula Vista, then dipped into a valley dotted by small houses, surrounded by gardens and orchards. Chickens roamed in many of the yards, scratching and pecking among the plants. Here and there, a man or woman, or sometimes a whole family worked the land, digging, chopping weeds or gathering crops.

Halfway up a slope, Carrie saw a large building with a sign advertising it as Redwood Hall. "That must be the clubhouse."

"Yes," Bertie replied. "It looks nice, doesn't it?"

"Do you know if they have a school yet?"

"I don't know, but they must." Mr. Owens let his eyes wander from the road to the surrounding land, then back to the road. "The community's been here about seven years. They must have built a school by now."

He drove leisurely through the town and turned east. "We'll keep to this road, find a picnic spot and have lunch somewhere." He pointed right. "The river is over there where the line of trees is growing. If you followed the river far enough, you'd arrive at the dam and the Otay Lakes Reservoir, but we won't go that far today."

As they left the community of Little Landers, houses and farms were farther apart, many of them situated on the slopes and hilltops, others nestled in the flat lands on either side of the river.

"There's a patch of trees over there," Bertie pointed out the car window. "That would make a nice place for a picnic."

"Yes, it would. Let me find a wide spot where I can park the car, and we'll walk over there." Mr. Owens slowed the car, pulled off the road and parked. They unloaded the lunch provisions, each of them carrying an item or two. It took about five minutes to reach the stand of trees. When they arrived, Bertie spread the blankets on the ground, and they settled onto them to enjoy their picnic.

After eating, Carrie walked farther on until she came to a stream bordered by brush. She poked her way through the branches but found the soil beneath her feet becoming more and more soggy. Deciding she had the wrong clothing for further adventures, she returned to where the Owenses sat on the blanket, each of them reading a book they had brought along. "I found a little stream over there," she told them.

"It's probably the river," Mr. Owens said as he looked up from his book. "It doesn't amount to much this time of year, but after a big rain, it sprawls all over the place. If I lived here, I'd make sure I lived on a hill, not down here where it could be flooded."

Bertie set her book in her lap. "I can see why people like to farm these bottom lands. The soil is rich and good."

Carrie lowered herself onto a corner of the blanket. "Have there been floods here in the past?"

"Not in the last four or five years, what with this drought going on," Mr. Owens said. "You mentioned a dam and a reservoir. Doesn't that provide enough water?" Carrie asked.

"Most the water from the reservoir goes to the Del Coronado hotel. A man over there pushed to get this dam built so the resort would have water. I suppose farmers get some of it. The troubling thing is that the water level in the reservoir is dropping."

"Who told you that, Archie?" Bertie asked.

"Various customers who come into the shop."

"And you believe all the talk that goes on in your barbershop?" Bertie teased him.

Mr. Owens grinned. "Not all of it, but when several people say the same thing, I pay attention."

They sat on the blanket, talking, for another half hour, then Bertie suggested they ought to start homeward. Since they had eaten most the food, there wasn't as much to carry on the return trip, and in a short while, they had the car loaded and were driving back down the valley through the community of Little Landers. The land stretched flat and wide to the southern end of San Diego Bay, where the tiny Otay river trickled into it. The bay curled northward toward the city of San Diego, then bent west to open into the Pacific Ocean.

It didn't take any time at all for Carrie and the Owenses to return home. As they unpacked the car, Carrie thanked both of them for including her in their outing. Bertie was the first one into the house while her husband and Carrie straggled along behind. Before they reached the porch, Mr. Owens stopped and turned toward Carrie. "Thank you for coming with us today. It helped keep our minds occupied on other things. You see, today is the anniversary of the day we lost our baby."

"I'm so sorry," Carrie exclaimed. "I had no idea you had suffered such a loss."

"He lived only a few days. Later, there were two miscarriages. Then we gave up hope. It's been very hard on Bertie."

Carrie felt tears rise to her eyes. "I can't imagine how difficult this has been. For both of you."

Mr. Owens sighed. "It's been hard." He walked slowly up the steps, his head hanging low. Raising it as he opened the front door, he entered the house, calling out, "What a wonderful day it's been! I love you, Bertie!"

Carrie followed him, set her parcels on the kitchen table; and as soon as possible, excused herself to go to her room. She sat on the edge of her bed thinking how the Owenses handled tragedy, comparing herself with them and questioning her way of dealing with adversity.

Chapter Fourteen

The weeks flew by. The weather cooled, but it was still dry. The drought became the main topic of conversation whenever people met each other in town or at church or social gatherings. Ranchers talked of taking out citrus trees that had died. Farmers monitored every drop of water they used on the vegetables and hoped for harvests adequate to take to market. Homeowners moaned about their wilting vegetables and flowers. Most ominous of all were the reports from the keepers of the Sweetwater and Otay River dams. Water levels in the reservoirs were reaching dangerously low levels. Everyone hoped the rains would come in the winter. Others urged prayer for rain.

A group of the latter organized a day of prayer at the Congregational Church the first day of November. Mrs. Owens was a member of the planning committee, and when she invited Carrie to the event, Carrie knew she must go in support of her friend, though she questioned how anyone could believe in prayer after losing three infants.

Committee members fanned out across the town, inviting and coercing every soul in town to "come and pray for rain." The sanctuary was full that night. Carrie slipped into a seat in the back row, followed minutes later by Mary. Carrie scooted over, wishing that anybody but Mary would sit next to her. She suppressed her thoughts about Mary by looking at other people, noting the ones she knew. Mr. and Mrs. Owens, together with the committee members, sat on the front row. Nate and his parents were in the place Carrie had seen them the first time she came to this church, near the front on the left-hand side. Nate's brother, James, and family took up most the row behind, Jennie looking over her shoulder to smile at Carrie. It looked like the families of all her students were there, except for David Imamura and his family. Carrie wasn't surprised because she'd been told that most Japanese were Buddhists and "didn't worship God like we do."

The minister gave a brief talk based on 2 Chronicles 7:14: "If my people who are called by my name, will humble themselves and pray and seek my face and turn from their wicked ways, then will I hear from heaven and will forgive their sin and will heal their land."

At the end of his homily, the pastor invited everyone to kneel and pray silently for a few minutes, to be followed by prayers from the mayor of Chula Vista, each of the committee members, and finally, himself. Carrie had never heard so many eloquent and lengthy prayers. Her legs ached from kneeling so long, and she prayed that the final "Amen" would come swiftly.

When it did, the minister invited everyone to stand and "leave this place filled with faith. Open your hymnals to page 195 and let's sing 'Showers of Blessing.'"

They filed out of the church into eighty-degree weather and cloudless skies. Carrie mingled with the crowd, making a point to meet as many of the parents of her students as possible. At the last, Jennie bounced up to Carrie with her friend, Sarah, who asked, "Miss Wyngate, when do you think God will send the rain?"

Carrie gulped. This was not a question that she could answer. Her faith, if she had any at all, was what she was sure others would label as "weak." She didn't want to express doubts to her students and searched for a suitable reply, cobbling together an answer that she hoped sounded spiritual.

"I think God will do it in His own time."

"What does that mean, Miss Wyngate?"

"Well, I think God is so big that we can't tell Him what to do or when to do it. We must wait on Him to do whatever He's going to do."

The girls nodded their heads and ran off, while Carrie congratulated herself on an answer that sounded far more spiritually mature than she knew herself to be.

"Good answer," a voice behind her said. She turned and saw Jennie's mother, Helen, standing behind her, the baby on her hip. "Children can ask tough questions, can't they?"

Carrie laughed. "I should say they can, and that one was out of my area of expertise."

Helen smiled. "That was quite a turnout for a prayer-meeting, wasn't it?"

"Yes, it was, though I haven't been to many prayer meetings, so I didn't know what to expect."

Helen shifted the baby to her other hip. "What most folks are expecting is rain."

"I sincerely hope they get it; but I'm not sure if God has much to do with such things."

"I know of one instance where He provided water."

"You do?"

"It happened about ten years ago. 1904, I think. A Christian woman by the name of Ellen White, who people say was a prophetess, was inspired to open a sanitarium in National City. You know where that is, don't you?"

"The town just north of us. Seems like the train came through there."

"East of town, on a nice slope, is where this Ellen and her friends found a large building and decided to buy it. She and a friend put up the money. There was only one problem: no water on the property."

"That sounds like a familiar problem for southern California," Carrie responded.

"Ellen hired a well driller and told him she had been shown that water could be found in a particular spot. She asked him to drill in that spot, and he did."

"And water gushed out?"

"No, it didn't. The well driller kept working. Still, no water. He wanted to quit and try another spot. Ellen kept telling him to continue right where he was. The man thought she was foolish, but since she insisted, he kept drilling."

"Sounds like Ellen was a very determined woman."

"She believed God had shown her where to find water, and she was right. The man struck a vein of water that has been constant ever since. It meets all the needs of the sanitarium and all the grounds. It's very pretty up there. You should see it sometime."

"Maybe I will, because I've never seen a miracle before."

Helen looked beyond Carrie and said, "Hello, Nate."

Carrie turned, saw Nate approaching and was startled to hear Helen say, "I was just telling Jennie's teacher about the well at the Paradise Valley Sanitarium. You should take her there sometime, Nate, so she can see it."

Nate mumbled something that might be construed as a yes or a maybe. Carrie wasn't sure, but as quickly as she could, she excused herself and walked away.

Later that evening, Mrs. Owens talked on and on about how successful the prayer meeting for rain had been. Carrie listened politely without making comments, not that Bertie needed encouragement to keep conversing. Eventually, Mr. Owens yawned and announced he was going to bed, providing an opportunity for Carrie to say goodnight, too. She climbed the stairs to her room, took off the locket from around her neck and set it next to the photograph of her and her grandmother. "What do you think," she asked of the picture, "about praying for rain?"

As she took off her clothes and put on her nightgown, she decided that if she ever got the opportunity to see the miracle well at the Sanitarium, she'd go. Alone. She didn't need Nate to take her.

Carrie climbed into bed, pulled the covers up to her chin, and the words she'd spoken earlier to Jennie and Sarah came back to her. God will do it in His own time....He is so big that we can't tell Him what to do or when to do it, but we should wait on Him....

Was it possible that somewhere deep inside she believed God would do something for her in His time? Judging from her past experiences, she doubted it. Yet, maybe miracles were still possible. There was that well of water....

Chapter Fifteen

As Thanksgiving Day approached, the Chula Vista Elementary School was busy preparing for the annual Thanksgiving program. Students learned lines about gratitude for bountiful harvests. Mothers stitched together costumes for Pilgrims and Indians. Mrs. England, the sixth-grade teacher who also doubled as the choir director, nearly lost her voice trying to bring music out of young throats. "Come, ye thankful people, come," they sang with varying degrees of skill.

In Carrie's classroom, cutouts of turkeys and pumpkins, colored with crayons, adorned the windows. She found creative ways to weave the history of America's pioneers into all the subjects. For penmanship, the children wrote a list of things they were thankful for. Arithmetic class consisted of studying measurements of the ingredients for pumpkin pie. If one pie required three quarters of a cup of sugar, how much sugar would it take for two pies?

At the end of one day, as the children left the classroom, David Imamura lingered and shyly came up to her desk. He seemed troubled. "Miss Wyngate, my parents don't think they should come to the program."

"Why is that, David?"

The boy looked at the floor, then up at her. "Because this is an American holiday and they are not Americans."

"Oh, David. Anybody can come to the Thanksgiving program. You tell your parents that in America, everyone is welcome."

David smiled and his eyes brightened, then he frowned. "They don't understand much English."

"But you do. You can explain it to them."

"Like I do when we go to the store?"

"Like you do wherever you go and your parents need help to understand."

"Thank you, Miss Wyngate. I will tell them they are most welcome and

I will explain everything!"

David left the room humming "Come Ye Thankful People, Come."

Carrie smiled. She felt a wave of gratitude overwhelm her that she had the happy occupation as a teacher in a country where there was freedom for all. She cleaned off her desk, put a few books in a bag to carry home and was about to leave the classroom for the day when Mr. Jenkins stopped by.

"Hello, Miss Wyngate. I'm making my rounds of all the teachers, seeing if everything is ready for the program this Thursday night. Is there anything else you need?" As he spoke, his eyes inspected her room.

"Thank you, Mr. Jenkins. I think everything's ready. The children are excited. I just hope they'll remember their lines; but if they don't, I'll be close by to prompt them."

"Isn't that being a crutch for them?"

"I don't think I understand what you mean, Mr. Jenkins."

"I mean, Miss Wyngate, that you shouldn't have to prompt children if you've adequately drilled them in memorization."

"The most adequately drilled students get nervous sometimes and forget. I'm there to help them if they need it."

"I see. These must be some of the new-fangled ideas being taught in normal school these days." He looked coldly at her. "You go right ahead and do it your way, but I demand you not to prompt my son with his lines. He needs no coddling."

Mr. Jenkins turned abruptly and left the room. As his footsteps pounded down the hallway, Carrie's hands began to tremble. She stood still for several minutes, trying to calm herself. Slowly, she walked out of the room, quietly closed the door and left the building. She wanted to scream and run and scream some more. On the other hand, she felt totally immobilized, like she couldn't move. Suddenly, she thought she understood why Charlie was always running, always moving; and at other times paralyzed into incapacity.

When she reached her house, she said a brief hello to Bertie and fled upstairs to think. Charlie had the second line in an acrostic poem about Thanksgiving that said, "H is for our homes so warm and bright." He and the group had repeated the whole poem flawlessly that morning during rehearsal. Surely, he wouldn't need a prompt. Yet she knew how children could fumble with an audience in front of them, and this audience would include a demanding father. What would happen if she needed to prompt the boy? She didn't know, but suddenly she lifted her chin and said, "I don't care what happens to me. I'll do what I have to do to help that boy.

Chapter Sixteen

Nate was walking down Third Avenue on his way to Shafer's hardware store. As he came upon City Hall, Mayor Rogers walked out. "Hello, Nate! You're just the man I'm looking for. We have a vacancy on the City Council and would like to appoint you for the rest of the term."

"Who, me? I don't think I'm qualified for that."

"Yes, you are. You know this town and you care about the community. We could use your ideas."

"Well....I don't know...."

"We wouldn't be asking you if we didn't think you could do it."

"Let me think about it."

"Sure, Nate. Think about it and give me an answer by tomorrow." The mayor shook his hand and stepped back inside City Hall.

Nate continued on his way, his head buzzing. Apparently, his face mirrored his mental astonishment because when he arrived at the hardware store, Mr. Shafer asked, "Something troubling you, Nate?"

Mr. Shafer listened as Nate told about the mayor's invitation.

"Can't think of anyone better suited for the job." The man slapped Nate on the shoulder. "Take it."

"I'm kind of young for such a position. Do you think people would listen to me?"

"There's only one way to earn people's respect, Nate. Be honest and responsible. From my observations, I'd say you've already got those traits."

"Thank you, Mr. Shafer. Now, before I forget it, I need to buy some screws." He fished in his pocket and held up one screw. "This size."

Mr. Shafer quickly found the screws, bagged them and Nate paid for them. As he left the hardware store, he said, "Thanks for your encouragement. I'll probably take that position. Maybe I can share some ideas I've had about how to make our city better."

"There you go, Nate. I know you'll do a fine job."

Nate walked rapidly back up Third Avenue, entered City Hall, found the mayor sitting at a desk and said, "I'll take the position, Mayor Rogers."

The mayor stood, leaned over his desk and shook Nate's hand. With a big smile, he said

"Good! Meetings are the second Tuesday evening of each month. See you right after Thanksgiving."

"Yes, sir."

Nate didn't know when he'd felt this good. What an honor! He couldn't wait to attend the first meeting. Maybe he'd have a chance to share some of his ideas for water conservation and for marketing the city. He reasoned with himself that he ought to keep a low profile and not promote his own ideas until he'd earned the respect of other council members. Even with the uncertainty of how someone his age might be received, he still felt excited.

Two days later, his name appeared in the newspaper, and wherever he went, people stopped and congratulated him, saying, "Just what we need—some young blood."

Of course his parents were proud of him. He'd expected that. His brother James teased, "I guess if you're old enough to shave, you're old enough to be on the City Council. I'm real proud of you, little brother."

Deep in his heart, Nate hoped Carrie would be proud of him, but he closed his ears to his heart and thought about the negative side of his new position. It was a volunteer one that didn't pay any money, and money is what he needed most. He constantly looked for odd jobs to pick up, such as working for other farmers to harvest their crops. Several widows in town had him on their lists as a handyman to repair broken windows, fallen fences or rotting steps. The school district had hired him as a part-time laborer during the construction of the new school, but that was over now. He also had the occasional job of delivery man for the railroad.

Nate was frugal and had a small savings account, but he was a long way from his goal of financial independence. It distressed him when he thought about it, so he kept busy.

There was always plenty to do in looking after the family farm. He kept a close eye on the fruit on the lemon trees. The crop looked fairly good despite the freeze of the winter before and the hot summer. On a wall calendar in the kitchen, Nate kept notes of when trees should be watered, fertilized, fumigated. He never varied from the schedule which he figured was one reason the crop looked as good as it did. With a little luck, and ample winter rains, the crops should yield some adequate income.

If the rains didn't come....Nate didn't want to think about it.

In his spare time, Nate snuck away to his wood-working corner of the barn. He was making toys for Christmas. For Jennie, he had built a doll cradle. It was all assembled but needed to be stained and rubbed into a smooth, satiny finish. For his nephew, he had carved a wooden truck with wheels that turned. He didn't know what to make for the baby. He'd look through some of his back issues of woodworking magazines and find something, but he needed to do it quickly. It was almost Thanksgiving.

That reminded him of the school program taking place in a couple of days. He and his parents would be there to cheer for his brother's children. Thinking of the upcoming school program made his thoughts turn to Carrie, and he wondered what songs and poems her classroom would be performing. He was sure it would be good. Carrie was that kind of person. She'd make sure every child had a part and did it well.

On Thursday night, Nate and his parents drove to the school and walked into the assembly room. Tonight would be the first program in the new school. It looked like everyone in town had noted that fact and was there. They wore their best clothes, chatting and laughing with one another, while children buzzed about, giggling at everything.

Nate and his parents sat next to James and his family near the front just behind the reserved section where school children sat waiting for their turn in the limelight. At 7:30 p.m., Mr. Jenkins climbed the stairs to the platform and stood in the middle of a world of wigwams constructed of canvas tarps scrounged from community barns. Behind him, on the back wall, a cabin had been painted on sheets of newsprint glued together. Shocks of corn stalks surrounded by pumpkins filled the corners of the platform.

He cleared his throat. "Family and friends, welcome to the first Thanksgiving program in our new school. The program will begin with presentations by the first grade and proceed, unannounced, grade by grade. Thank you for coming. Let the show begin!"

Loud applause erupted, then stilled as the first-graders took their places on the platform. Mary shepherded them into place. Nate noticed how nice Mary looked in a brown skirt and white shirtwaist, a braided belt accentuating her slim waist.

When the second grade came on, James' son, Paul, tromped to the middle of the stage dressed in buckskin pants, brown shirt and a headdress made from chicken feathers. Nate and family cheered loudly.

Each grade did similar things: a poem, a song, a dramatization of the first Thanksgiving. When Carrie's class took the stage, she lined twelve of the students in the front, the rest in the back, then took her place behind a side curtain. Nate could see only the edge of her skirt and her feet, but he figured she was there to help the children in case anyone's memory faltered.

The first of the twelve children was David Imamura, who took one step forward and recited in a clear voice, "T is for our thankfulness for many joys and blessings." He stepped back, and Charlie stepped forward.

"H is for our...our...H is for our...." The boy looked like a scared rabbit. He stared at the floor, scuffed his feet and began again. "H is for...." Almost frantically, Charlie looked to the side where Carrie stood. Nate surmised that Carrie prompted him, because the boy turned back to the audience and spoke rapidly, but faintly. "H is for our homes so warm and bright."

After the program, Nate saw Mr. Jenkins approach Carrie. He had an angry-looking face. Nonchalantly, Nate wandered in the direction of the two, getting close enough to hear Mr. Jenkins say, "You defied my order. Young lady, I am reporting you to the school board." Carrie opened her mouth to say something, but Mr. Jenkins had already turned from her and stomped away.

Nate moved in. "What was that about?"

Carrie's face looked pale, and her lower lip trembled as she began telling Nate about Mr. Jenkins' demand that she do nothing to help his son if he needed it. "I couldn't leave that boy floundering, not when I'd told all the children I'd be right there to prompt them if they needed it."

Nate's jaw tightened, and he pounded a fist into his other hand.

Carrie twisted her hands together. "I defied him. He has a right to call me on that."

Nate said nothing for a second or two. "You defied the principal. In this case, I'm glad you did." He kept his eyes on hers. "Where do we go from here?"

"He says he's taking it to the school board."

Nate looked down at her, noticing how fragile yet strong and beautiful she looked. "That's exactly where I'm taking the matter. To the school board."

"What?"

"My brother, James, is a member of the school board. I'm talking to him about this."

Nate walked away, leaving Carrie standing there, still feeling shaky. Shortly, some of her students surrounded her, and she began praising each one for the excellent job they did. At the edge of the group, she saw David standing with his parents and a younger sister. The parents wore those billowy pantaloon-like garments with tunics on top that she'd seen on the Japanese people working in their gardens. As soon as the children dispersed, David escorted his parents to her. "Miss Wyngate, these are my parents." Then he said something in Japanese which ended with the words "Miss Carolyn Wyngate." She was about to extend her hand to them for a handshake, but they immediately bowed to her, so she bowed back.

"It's a pleasure to meet you, Mr. and Mrs. Imamura."

They said something in Japanese and bowed again. David translated, "They say they are happy to meet the teacher of their son."

Carrie touched David on the arm. "Tell them I am pleased to have such a fine student in my classroom."

David blushed, hesitated, then translated to them. They smiled and bowed again. "Please tell them," Carrie continued, "that I'm happy they came to our program. They are always welcome to come to school functions."

David translated again, and once more, his parents bowed. Carrie bowed. Everyone smiled and nodded as they parted from each other.

Carrie watched the Imamuras leave the auditorium and thought what a nice ending they had brought to a difficult evening. At the back of the room, she saw Nate talking to his brother. Both of them looked her way, then continued their conversation. She hoped something good would come of the connection she had with the Landons. It was the only hope she had.

Chapter Seventeen

The Thanksgiving holiday gave Carrie a much-needed rest. She loved teaching but felt grateful for time off to regain her energy, particularly after the confrontation with Mr. Jenkins.

For a few days, school-related things could be forgotten. Since Carrie had nowhere to go and no family to celebrate with, the Owenses welcomed her to their Thanksgiving dinner. They also invited four other people from the community, folk who had no families in Chula Vista.

The day before, Carrie helped Bertie make two pumpkin pies, two apple pies and a sheet of dinner rolls. The next day, they rose early to stuff the turkey and put it in the oven. Carrie peeled potatoes while Bertie prepared a pan of sweet potatoes topped with marshmallows, brown sugar and toasted pecans. They continued their dinner preparations by grinding fresh cranberries and oranges for a relish, pouring cream and a large dollop of butter into the white potatoes and mashing them to a creamy mound. Carrie set the table with Bertie's best dinnerware and the silverware that had been polished the previous afternoon. By the time the guests arrived at 1 p.m., Bertie was stirring the gravy and keeping an eye on a pot of green beans and a smaller pan of corn.

It was a feast that left them all sleepy. They retired to the living room, where Mr. Owens and the two male guests immediately fell asleep in their chairs. The women nodded their heads a couple of times but revived themselves so they wouldn't miss any opportunities to talk. Carrie listened for awhile, then excused herself to take a walk.

The weather didn't feel like Thanksgiving. In Chicago at this time of year, it would be cold. Here, it was seventy degrees with a few scattered clouds in the sky. As Carrie walked along the edge of the unpaved street, she noticed that the plants, bushes, even the lemon trees were dusty, and she wondered how long it had been since it rained. Apparently, quite a while. There hadn't been any rain since she came at the end of August.

A car stopped beside her. It was Miguel with two teen-aged girls. Carrie hadn't seen him since the Saturday night at Balboa Park. "Hello, Miss Carrie." His dark eyes sparkled. "Are you going anywhere in particular?"

"No. Just getting some fresh air."

"Well, hop in and let me take you to some real fresh air. I'm taking my sister and her friend to the beach. Come with us."

Carrie could think of no excuse to decline his invitation. It was a holiday. She couldn't claim that she needed to go to school or to the store. "I'd better tell the Owenses where I'm going so they won't worry about me."

"Fine. I'll drive you back there." He did, and Carrie stepped into the house to find that the guests had departed. Mr. and Mrs. Owens sat quietly, talking with each other. They smiled and nodded when she told them where she was going and with whom. She went to her room and picked up a jacket.

Back in Miguel's car, Carrie studied him more closely than she had before. He had black hair, slicked back from his dark face, and a smile made particularly noticeable because of the contrast of white teeth against beige skin. A slight accent gave his voice a pleasing lilt.

Miguel drove south of Chula Vista, then turned west toward a small town on the edge of the ocean. "This is Imperial Beach," he explained. "We'll park here and walk toward that pier over there."

As soon as he stopped the car, his sister and friend jumped out and walked the opposite direction from Carrie and Miguel.

Miguel pointed straight ahead, and Carrie saw a long pier jutting into the ocean. Waves rolled in gently, slapping the pilings, then spilling themselves onto the white sand. A number of people walked on the beach; others walked on the pier or leaned themselves against the rail.

Miguel looked at Carrie. "I want you to see the wave machine on the end of the pier."

She squinted her eyes. "A wave machine? You have to have a machine to make waves?"

Miguel laughed. "No. It's supposed to catch the energy of the waves and turn it into electricity. Some man invented it, and several ocean piers along the coast have them."

"That's quite an idea. How's it working?

"I really don't know," Miguel said as he bent over and took off his shoes. "It's easier to walk in the sand barefoot," he explained, so Carrie took her shoes off. The sand felt soft on her feet as they walked toward the pier. Nearest the shore, the sand was wet and hard and felt cold.

"I heard you're from Chicago. I bet you don't walk on the beach on Thanksgiving Day in Chicago."

"There's a beach along Lake Michigan; but you're right, it's usually too cold this time of year to walk on it." The breeze off the Pacific hit Carrie's face. She was glad she'd brought a jacket. "Miguel, I think I'd like to walk on the beach before we go onto the pier."

"Fine with me. We'll come back to the pier later."

"Where did you grow up, Miguel?"

"Right here in Chula Vista. My parents are from Mexico. They came here before I was born."

"Do you speak both languages?"

Miguel looked at Carrie, his eyes teasing her. "Si, Señorita."

His voice sounded mellow, and she liked the way he rolled the r. "Spanish is a nice-sounding language. I think I'd like to learn it."

"I could teach you."

He was too quick—too eager. Mentally, Carrie pulled away from him, not responding to his offer. Knowing his eyes were on her, she kept her eyes focused straight ahead. That's when she saw a familiar figure. Two familiar figures: Nate and Mary, in the distance, walking toward them. Carrie's heart pounded. She couldn't turn around. Miguel would think it odd; besides, he, too, had just recognized the approaching pair.

"There's Nate and Mary." Miguel quickened his stride, Carrie following, until they were within a few feet of the couple. Carrie noticed the surprised look on Nate's face and wondered if her face registered the same. She turned her eyes away from him and fixed them on Mary.

"I thought you were going home for Thanksgiving."

Mary tossed her head, grinning up at Nate, who kept his gaze on Carrie and Miguel. "My parents both got sick with bad colds. I didn't want to expose myself to something that would knock me out of teaching for several days, so I stayed in Chula Vista."

"I'm sorry. You should have said something. You could have had dinner with me and the Owenses."

"Nate's brother, James, rescued me. He's one of the school board members who always looks after the teachers, making sure they're not alone on holidays. He invited me to their home for dinner." Mary tossed her head, making the curls around her face bounce. "After dinner, we all decided to come to the beach."

Carrie didn't know what to say but didn't have to say anything because at that moment, Jennie came running toward her. "Hi, Miss Wyngate!"

Hugging the girl, she said, "Hi, Jennie! What a nice surprise to find you at the beach."

James, carrying baby Joseph, his wife, Helen, beside him, walked toward them. The younger brother, Paul, skipped ahead of them. They all crowded around, and Carrie introduced Miguel to James' family. For some time, they all stood and visited, then James said it was time to round up the children and get them home before dark. They walked as a group across the sand toward their respective vehicles. Carrie was walking beside Helen, when James said in a low voice, "Nate told me Mr. Jenkins is bringing up an incident that involves you at the next school board."

Carrie looked around to make sure no one else in the group was listening. Miguel was ahead, walking beside Nate and Mary; the children were running way ahead of them all. She looked at James and saw concern in his eyes.

"I just want you to know, I'm supporting you," he said.

Carrie blinked to hold back the tears that suddenly rose in her eyes. "Thank you, James. I really appreciate that."

They walked in silence for several minutes. Miguel turned his back on Nate and Mary and came to her, whispering "I still want to take you out on the pier."

Before she had time to answer, he shouted "Hey, everybody! Carrie and I want to walk out on the pier, so we'll say 'adios' for now."

They parted from the group, and Carrie reluctantly walked with Miguel to the pier. The sun was moving toward the horizon, making people's shadows long in the sand.

"Let's stay and watch the sunset," Miguel urged.

They stood at the end of the pier, leaning against the rail, looking west where the sun hovered a few inches above the ocean horizon. The clouds were tinged in pink and gold. Waves whispered against the pilings of the pier. Gulls wheeled and glided above them. The wind felt chilly, and Miguel moved closer to her, slipping his arm around her. His warmth felt good, but she pulled away, keeping her eyes on the sun. The bottom edge of it clipped the horizon, then half of it disappeared. Quickly and finally, the sun dropped into the ocean, swaths of mauve and gold in the sky reflected in the wet sand.

"The sun's gone down, so we'd better go now."

"What's the rush? Don't you like it here with me?" Miguel looked at her, but Carrie had already turned to go.

"Wait, Carrie! I've got to find the girls."

Chapter Eighteen

Classes resumed on Monday. The children were bubbling with energy, except for Charlie. He was unusually quiet. Carrie tried to draw him out, but he didn't respond. Undoubtedly, his father had come down on him for his lapse of memory at the Thanksgiving program. That was ten days ago. He should have been over it by now; although she had to admit, she wasn't. The prospect of facing school board action filled Carrie with anxiety. Perhaps some of her angst could be relieved if she knew when the school board met. Maybe Mary would know.

An opportunity to ask came during the lunch hour, when Carrie found Mary on the school grounds watching over her first-graders. They chatted a few minutes about nothing in particular, then Carrie asked, "I've been wondering, when does the school board meet?"

"Why do you want to know?"

"Just wondering. You seem to have a real in with the school board—at least one of them."

"The last Monday of each month, except this month is December and that would be during the holidays, so it's postponed until January."

"Oh."

Mary touched Carrie's arm, causing Carrie to turn and see the mischievous glint in Mary's eyes. "That was interesting, running into you and Miguel on the beach," Mary said, a sly grin tipping up the corners of her mouth.

"Quite the coincidence." Carrie didn't want to talk about it, so she terminated the conversation. "I've got to get inside and set up some things for the afternoon reading class."

When school let out for the day and all her students had filed out of the classroom, David lingered behind and came toward her. "Miss Wyngate, may I tell you something?"

"Of course, David. What is it?"

David shifted from one foot to the other. "I don't know if I should tell." He wrinkled his forehead and bit his lip. "You have to keep it a secret."

"Alright, David."

"It's about Charlie."

"Oh." Carrie waited for David to continue.

"His dad was real mad at him because he forgot his part in the Thanksgiving program."

Carrie stayed calm, though she felt her throat tighten. "And you wanted me to know because....."

"Because I thought maybe you could fix it so he doesn't have to say anything at the Christmas program."

Carrie wanted to throw her arms around David but restrained herself. "That's very thoughtful of you to think of that. I'll see what I can do."

David smiled and said, "Thanks, teacher. I'll see you tomorrow." He turned and ran out the door, leaving Carrie to consider how to use this information.

If all the students had lines to memorize and Charlie didn't, the boy would feel left out. How could she put together a program that would include him and still protect him?

The answer came when Mrs. England, the music teacher, stopped by an hour later as Carrie sat at her desk grading papers.

"Do you have a minute, Miss Wyngate?"

"Of course."

"I'm arranging the Christmas program and had some ideas I wanted to run past you."

Carrie smiled. "Good! Because I don't have any."

"I was thinking that instead of each grade doing poems and songs independently of the other classrooms, that we'd have a more unified program if I planned it and made the assignments of which students would do what."

"That's fine by me," Carrie answered. "What do you have in mind?"

"Telling the Christmas story, of course; and I thought maybe the fourth graders could be the angel choir."

"That's a good idea! Do you want any of them to say anything?"

"No. I've asked some fifth-graders to be shepherds. They'll do the speaking parts. All your students will have to do is dress in costumes that resemble angels and sing a song that has 'Glory to God in the highest' in it. Do you think your pupils will go for that?"

"I don't know how they'll feel about it, but it sounds like a great idea to me because it relieves me of helping them memorize poems."

"They'll have to memorize the words and music to the song, but that's my responsibility since I'm the choir director."

Carrie smiled and said ,"You're an answer to prayer."

"How's that?"

Not wanting to divulge what was behind her remark, Carrie simply shrugged her shoulders and kept smiling. "I didn't know what I was going to do for the Christmas program. You came along and solved the problem."

After Mrs. England left, Carrie reviewed their conversation, marveling how the proposed program would rescue Charlie from further embarrassment or displeasure from his father. She also wondered what had prompted her to talk of answered prayer when she was a person who didn't believe in it. Or did she?

Chapter Nineteen

On December 9, 1915, Charles Hatfield, a rainmaker who had acquired a reputation in his ability to produce rain in various parts of the country, made a proposal to the San Diego City Council.

"I will fill the Morena Reservoir to overflowing between now and next December 20, 1916, for the sum of $10,000, in default of which I ask no compensation."

It was the fifth year of drought. Morena Reservoir, which supplied the city of San Diego, was uncomfortably low. Otay Reservoir was almost empty. The council voted four to one to authorize Hatfield to fulfill his promise.

The news spread quickly and pitted citizens against each other with reactions of "Foolishness!" to "Scientific" to "We'll wait and see." Members of the Chula Vista City Council who met the following Tuesday were equally divided.

As a newcomer to the Council, Nate didn't say anything but told himself he would do some research about Hatfield, his credentials and his "science," if it could be called that. If it were based on credible knowledge, it could be a life-saving venture for the community. If it were a hoax, it would be a personal disappointment to every person in southern California.

Nate sincerely hoped Hatfield was not an unscrupulous charlatan. He talked it over with his father later that evening.

"When we lived in Kansas," his father began, "we had droughts, and there were some men who claimed they had chemical formulas that would entice rain. There may be something to this. I'd like to know more about Mr. Hatfield and his methods."

Nate agreed. Just then, his mother entered the room. She had obviously overheard their conversation because she said, "Ridiculous! What we need to do is trust in God, not some voodoo with his witchcraft."

"Now, Agnes," Nate's father began in a quiet voice. "It's possible that

Mr. Hatfield could be working with scientific principles."

Mrs. Landon was adamant. "A waste of time. We'd be better served spending the time praying to God for rain."

Nate wanted to remind his mother that they'd had a prayer meeting for rain two months earlier and nothing had come of it. He chose to keep his thoughts to himself.

The next morning, Nate met with his brother, and the two of them discussed the Hatfield proposal. James explained his stance "Let the man try his magic. If it works, great! If it doesn't, we haven't lost anything by letting him try."

"That's kind of how I look at it," Nate agreed, "though I'd like to know more about the man's methods."

"Maybe we could hike up to the Morena Reservoir when Hatfield starts work and have a chat with the man."

"That's quite a ways, and I don't know when Hatfield begins."

"I'm sure the newspaper will keep us informed. Meanwhile, I've been thinking about what you told me about Mr. Jenkins' accusation against Miss Wyngate. The school board will be meeting next month. Do you think I should talk with her and get her side of the story?"

"That's an idea. Has Mr. Jenkins filed an official complaint with the board?" Nate asked.

"Not that I know of."

"In that case, it might be premature to talk with her. What if he doesn't file a complaint and drops the issue? That would be distressful to Carrie... uh...Miss Wyngate."

"Are you on a first-name basis with her?" James teased.

Nate shrugged his shoulders and tried to sound nonchalant. "I picked her up at the train station when she arrived in town. We got acquainted."

"I see." James paused. "Seriously, Nate, she's a nice person. Pretty, too. Jennie almost worships her as a teacher."

Nate avoided looking at his brother, choosing to stare into the distance.

"It's about time you thought of settling down, finding someone...."

"And what might I have to offer a woman? A room in my parent's house? Got to get some money together, which is mighty hard to do with this drought ruining crops and lives. Personally, I hope Mr. Hatfield can make rain. I don't care how he does it."

Nate stomped off.

Later in the day, he sat in his room looking at a balance sheet he had created for the expenses and potential income from the lemon orchard. Until the harvest, he gloomily thought, there was no income. He had a small personal savings account at the bank, but he hadn't been able to deposit any money in it for a long time.

Carrie sat at her desk in the classroom grading papers. She worked her way through a stack of arithmetic assignments, set her pencil down and looked out the window. December 16 and the weather looked like summer. Her mind wandered back to Chicago. She was five years old. Snow was falling. Her father had promised to help her build a snowman when he came home from work. He never came.

Carrie shook her head to clear the memory. Memories hurt. She avoided them. Pushing her chair away from the desk, she stood, walked to the coat rack in the back of the room and picked off a jacket. A jacket is all you need in December? She had a red snowsuit with matching red mittens. She would wear it when she and Daddy....

Throwing the jacket over her shoulders, Carrie walked quickly out of the classroom and shut the door behind her. In the hallway, she met Mary.

"Hello, Carrie. You look sad. Anything wrong?"

Carrie hated that she was so poor at disguising her feelings. "I was having a touch of nostalgia thinking about Chicago. We usually had snow this time of year. Look at it here. Warm. Dry. How can you have Christmas without snow?"

"Guess you'll soon find out," Mary remarked as she switched her book bag from one hand to the other. "We get snow in the mountains, except not for the last four years with this drought."

"Let's hope it rains this winter," Carrie said as the two of them walked toward the front door.

Mary pushed open the door and asked, "Have you heard about the rainmaker the city of San Diego hired?"

"Yes. He's either a genius or a fool."

"I thought you, a teacher with inquiring mind, would be looking at it from a scientific viewpoint." Mary spoke with a teasing lilt to her voice.

"I am," Carrie said as she thrust her arms into her jacket. "I'm just waiting to see the scientific evidence."

"Why don't we dance for rain?" Mary joked as she moved her feet in a two-step movement. "Or we could hire a magician. Do whatever it takes to get rain, is what I say. Even pray."

Carrie didn't know whether to gasp or laugh. She chose to laugh because that's the effect Mary always had on her. One couldn't stay too serious, or jealous, around a person who always saw the fun in life.

Carrie was still smiling when they parted at the corner of Third and F, Mary going toward her residence and Carrie walking to the pharmacy to buy some aspirin. She'd been having headaches lately. A number of things worried her, sometimes woke her in the night. Charlie and his father. The upcoming school board meeting. The blast of memories she experienced a few minutes ago in her classroom. What did it all mean? She left Chicago with every intention of never returning to it—not even in her thoughts, and especially not in her emotions. Hiding her feelings, refusing to acknowledge them, seemed to be the safest way to live. Except it wasn't working as well as she'd planned.

As she came to the pharmacy, the door opened and Mr. Owens exited. "Hello, Carrie!"

"Hello, Mr. Owens."

"Say, Carrie, I'm sure you've heard about this Mr. Hatfield that San Diego is hiring to make rain."

"Yes. Most interesting and unusual."

"It is. Seems like it's got the whole town divided. What do you think about it?"

"I'm not sure. I think I need more information."

"That's what I think, and that's what I was telling Bertie, but she's convinced the man is a fake and all we need to do is get right with God and pray."

Carrie smiled. "I can imagine her saying that."

"She's my wife and I love her to death, but she's not very open-minded sometimes."

Carrie shrugged. "I guess we all have our quirks, Mr. Owens. I'm glad you told me how she feels. I'll not bring up the subject to her."

"That might be wise." Mr. Owens said. "Well, I've got to get back to work. I'll see you this evening."

When Carrie walked into the pharmacy, there were two customers arguing loudly about Mr. Hatfield.

"I tell you, the man's a con artist."

"They say he's been successful in producing rain in other parts of the country."

"Where?"

"Los Angeles. Fresno. He's done a lot of scientific study on the subject.
"

"False science. A bunch of magic tricks."

"Gentlemen, gentlemen," Mr. Walsh intervened. "You need to take your argument outside. I've got customers to serve. What can I do for you, Miss?"

He turned his eyes on Carrie, who said, "I need a bottle of aspirin."

"I think I do, too. People have been coming in and out of here all day, arguing about Mr. Hatfield. It's enough to give me a headache."

The two men walked outside, talking loudly as they went. "What a waste of time and money for a man to fiddle with the elements—the God-created elements."

"But what if his methods work?"

"He ought to pack his bags right now and go back to wherever he came from."

The door closed on their argument. Carrie made her purchase and left the store, not knowing whether to laugh or cry at the debate waging in Chula Vista about a man who claimed he could make it rain.

Suddenly, she wondered what Nate thought of Mr. Hatfield. Since he was on the Chula Vista City Council, he must have an opinion. Maybe he has information the rest of us don't have. I'd like to talk to him about it. Then, she wondered why it should matter to her what Nate Landon thought about Mr. Hatfield.

Chapter Twenty

With Christmas ten days away, Charles Hatfield took a back seat in the minds of Chula Vistans. Everyone was busy preparing for the holiday. City workers wound garlands around poles in the business district. This is where Carrie came upon Nate one afternoon. He stood on a ladder with a rope of greenery draped over his shoulder.

"Hello! Is this part of your City Council duties?"

"I think this is one of the jobs they assign to younger members," he said from the top of the ladder. "Older men wouldn't want to do this."

"You're doing a great job. Looks festive. By the way, congratulations on your position on the City Council."

"Thank you."

She walked on past store windows with holly wreaths, display cases filled with toys and Santa Claus figures. The Congregational Church had a nativity scene on the front lawn, and the post office had a red banner urging people to mail their gifts before December 20.

The thought popped into her head that she had no one to mail a package to or anyone who would be sending her a greeting card. It depressed her, and she forced herself to smile. She must keep up the appearance of Christmas cheer.

Carrie had done her best in decorating her classroom. Her pupils had cut out strips of red and green construction paper, glued together into circles, to form long chains that she hung from one wall to the next. The children made paper snowflakes and pasted them on the windows. Jennie's father brought a small Christmas tree, and she and her students had strung it with popcorn strands and clumps of silver tinsel. Gifts were piling up underneath it, the result of a name drawing.

Wired with anticipation and enthusiasm, the children could hardly wait for the distribution of gifts that would be the climax of the school Christmas program on the 22nd.

Under Mrs. England's tutelage, the fourth-grade angel choir was edging toward musical perfection. Less than two weeks before the program, Mrs. England decided that her plan for a totally musical program might not be enough. She ran around to the upper-grade classrooms and solicited a few students with unusual memory talent. Two eighth-graders had been enlisted to deliver "Twas the Night Before Christmas." Three sixth-graders were rounded up to recite a piece about Christmas Eve mice stealing Santa Claus' cookies. They would dress in grey costumes with long tails. A seventh-grader volunteered that she knew some lines from Charles Dickens. Mrs. England slated her to begin the program:

"I am sure that I have always thought of Christmas time, when it has come round...as a good time: a kind, forgiving, charitable, pleasant time; the only time I know of, in the long calendar of the year, when men and women seem by one consent to open their shut-up hearts freely."

The hall was packed with parents, grandparents, aunts and uncles on the evening of the twenty-second. Carrie looked across the auditorium just as the Owenses walked in. Hurrying toward them, she said "What a surprise! I'm so glad you came."

"We don't usually come to school programs," Mr. Owens said as he put his arm around his wife. Bertie had a stiff, unnatural smile on her face.

"We've heard so much about the school programs that we thought we'd come and see what all the fuss is about." Mr. Owens looked around the room. "I must say, this new school is mighty nice."

"It's a real pleasure to teach here."

"That's the other reason we came." Mr. Owens' eyes twinkled. "We keep hearing about the wonderful fourth-grade teacher."

Carrie stammered, "Thank you. Don't know if I'm deserving of any praise. The children are the ones who are amazing." She pointed toward the left front of the room. "There are a few vacant seats over there. If you'll excuse me, I need to be with my students. Enjoy the evening."

The program went well, aside from a shepherd stepping on the robe of another and causing him to stumble. The headgear of one of the wise men slid down over his eyes. He pushed it up and continued his journey to the manger. A nervous poetry speaker rushed through his lines so fast it sounded like one long, incomprehensible word. "Twas-the-night-before-Christmas-and-all-through-the house...."

Not all the voices in the fourth-grade choir reached the high notes in "Hark, the Herald Angels Sing" but they all looked quite cherubic in their angel robes.

One could feel the energy level in the auditorium rising as the program neared its close. Children squirmed in their seats in anticipation of the arrival of Santa Claus. They screamed with excitement as he walked down the center aisle with a bulky pack over his shoulder. The older students knowingly whispered to each other that the man was one of their fathers. Santa Claus enlisted some helpers and within a half hour, all the gifts had been distributed, one for each child. In closing, Mr. Jenkins announced that every child could come forward and take one of the mesh stockings hanging on the tree. Within minutes, the tree had been stripped bare, and children were digging through a variety of nuts in their Christmas stockings to pull out the hard candies. which they popped in their mouths.

Carrie made her way through the crowd. Parents kept stopping to thank her for her work as a teacher, which made her feel good. By the time she stepped outside, she walked alone. She took a deep breath of the evening air and forced herself to keep her head high and a pleasant expression on her face. She dreaded tomorrow. It would be Christmas Eve. Earlier in the week, Bertie had asked her to help decorate their tree. It was the last thing Carrie wanted to do. Then, she considered how difficult this time of year must be for a childless woman. Yet, Bertie had come to the program. If she can do it, I can do it.

The next morning, she awoke early with a task in mind: buy gifts for Mr. and Mrs. Owens. Right after breakfast, she slipped a light jacket on, grabbed her purse and headed for the general store on Third Avenue. As soon as she walked in, she saw Nate. He was paying for some purchases and didn't see her. She thought of slipping back out the door before he saw her. It didn't work. He turned from the counter and walked straight toward her. They greeted each other and stood facing each other as if they had something to say but couldn't put it into words. Finally, Carrie asked, "What do you think about Mr. Hatfield and his offer to fill up the reservoir?"

"What do you think?" he countered.

"I'm not sure if he's a fake, a magician or a bona fide scientist, so I'm taking the 'wait-and-see' approach." She shrugged her shoulders.

Nate rubbed his chin with his hand. "That's pretty much my thoughts about it. I'm trying to find more information about the man."

"Would you be so kind as to share what you find out? Because if it's based on solid science, I want to know."

"Me, too." Nate looked out the window. "Our region needs rain, and if he can help solve the problem, he'll be a hero."

Carrie stepped to one side to take up a search of the aisles for gifts for the Owens. Nate stood aside and let her pass. She heard the bell on the door tinkle as he opened it and left. Her mind went with him. Halfheartedly, she scanned the shelves for suitable gifts. Finally, she picked out a small yellow ceramic pot for Bertie, hoping the woman would be pleased with a new container for one of her plants. A box of monogrammed handkerchiefs seemed like a good gift for Mr. Owens. She bought wrapping paper and ribbon as well, paid for her purchases and left. Outside, Nate was waiting for her.

Unable to hide her surprise, she asked, "You're still here?"

"Yes. There's something I'd like to talk to you about. Mind if I walk along with you a little way?"

"No, not at all." Carrie kept her eyes straight ahead but felt Nate watching her.

"You're doing a great job as a teacher." He paused. "I've heard many parents say good things about you."

Her cheeks turned warm. "Thank you. I'm glad to hear it."

Nate stopped walking, so she did, too. He faced her. "The thing is, I can't figure out why Mr. Jenkins feels the way he does about you. He's been the principal for five years. I never heard him having troubles with teachers before. It doesn't make sense."

Carrie sighed. "No, it doesn't, unless the man is trying to hide something and feels like I could expose him."

"What?"

"The way he treats his son. He's abusive. I'm sure of it, but can't prove it.

And if I could, would anybody care? Most people feel they shouldn't stick their noses into other folks' parenting styles."

Carrie stopped and took a deep breath before continuing. "I learned some things in normal school about children like Charlie."

"Is he different in some way?"

"The research is just beginning, but there are indications that students like Charlie have a hard time learning things in the usual way. Many parents and teachers don't understand this. They get frustrated and angry. I think that's what's wrong with Mr. Jenkins."

Nate looked thoughtful. "Hmmm" is all he said.

"Charlie needs help and understanding. So does his father. This thing could blow up into something big at the school board. That wouldn't help anybody."

"I'm afraid I don't have any solutions. I know my brother James wants to help you, but he doesn't know what to do, either."

"Maybe we should form a prayer committee." Carrie's voice sounded calloused, even to herself.

Nate stared at her. "That sounded cynical."

"Maybe that's what I am. It's hard to be a believer when God has let you down."

"What do you mean by that? You sound bitter about something."

Carrie sneered. "Oh, now I'm bitter as well as cynical."

"I didn't mean it in a bad way. I wanted to help...if I can. Obviously, I can't."

"Thank you, Mr. Landon, for your diagnosis of my problems. I've got to be going." She brushed past him and stalked down the street. He turned in the opposite direction.

Chapter Twenty-one

Carrie stomped home, her feet slapping hard against the road. Nate's words made her angry, then troubled. Had she really become a bitter woman? When she opened the front door of the Owenses' home, her face must have revealed the turmoil inside because Bertie looked up and said, "You look a little gloomy for Christmas Eve. Come, help me decorate the tree. That'll cheer you up."

Carrie opened her mouth to deny her feelings. Her mind stopped her with the thought that Bertie had accumulated heavy losses but had not turned into a bitter unbeliever. Immediately, Carrie pasted a smile on her face.

"Let me put my things away upstairs. I'll be right back to help you."

Together, the two women lifted fragile glass balls out of boxes and placed them on the tree. There were hand-carved decorations too—fat little Santa Clauses, angels and stars. They were draping tinsel over the tree when Mr. Owens came home. "Looks beautiful. You two have done a fine job."

"Thank you, Honey. Would you mind lighting a fire in the fireplace?"

"Are you sure? It's hardly cold enough outside for a fire. We'll be too hot."

"A fire makes it more Christmasy."

Mr. Owens walked into the kitchen and out the back door. He came back with a load of wood in his arms. He was setting it down in a wooden box next to the fireplace when someone knocked on the front door. Bertie answered.

"Merry Christmas, Mr. Landon!"

Carrie's head jerked toward the door. The last person she wanted to see right now was Nate Landon. It wasn't Nate. It was James and he stepped toward her and said, "Miss Wyngate, I came to invite you to Christmas dinner at our home tomorrow."

Immediately, Carrie remembered what Mary had told her about James Landon always looking after teachers who had no place to go on a holiday. She didn't like the feeling of being the lonely teacher to be pitied.

"Thank you, Mr. Landon, but I had planned to be with the Owenses tomorrow."

"Oh, go on, Carrie. Accept the invitation. Archie and I will be fine with just the two of us." Bertie winked at her husband and he winked back.

Carrie hesitated. Nate would surely be there, and their conversation the day before still rankled her.

"My parents and brother will also be joining us. Do come. Jennie will be so thrilled to have her teacher."

Carrie had many reasons to decline the invitation but didn't know how to do so gracefully. The fact that James was on the school board played into her final decision.

"I'd be happy to come to your home for Christmas dinner. I could come a little early and give your wife a hand."

"Good. I'll come by and pick you up around noon."

After James left, both Bertie and her husband talked about how nice it was that Carrie had an invitation to dinner from the Landon family. Carrie suspected that the Owenses' real joy lay in their desire to connect her with Nate.

Mr. Owens knelt on the hearth, laid a fire and lit it. Soon, the flames flickered, casting a warm glow to the room and creating sparkly spots on the glass ornaments. The faint scent of pine filled the air. Carrie closed her eyes and took a deep breath. She was back in Chicago in her grandmother's apartment looking at their small Christmas tree and feeling such a deep loneliness that it made her chest and stomach hurt. "It's just you and me now," she heard her grandmother say. "But we'll have a nice Christmas."

Carrie's eyes flew open. No, we won't have a nice Christmas. There'll never be another nice Christmas. Not without Daddy.

"Please excuse me," Carrie heard herself say to the Owenses. "I need to go to my room."

She flung herself across the bed, ready to cry, but the tears that should have come were too deeply buried to surface. Her mind replayed her losses. A mother gone before she ever knew her. A father taken before Christmas. Grandma swept away by a stroke. All of them gone. Gone! Carrie pounded the pillow and said between clenched teeth, "And Nate wonders why I'm bitter."

Twisting the pillow in her hands, she recounted the most recent loss—the one that propelled her out of Chicago. It made her angry at her own vulnerabilities. Angry at the justice system. Angry at...Carrie stopped herself.

She lay still, closed her eyes and willed the irritation to drain out of her. Finally, she rolled over and stared at the ceiling, feeling like a rag doll that had been pulled back and forth between two toddlers. It shocked her that Christmas had brought out such intense feelings. How will I make it through the whole holiday?

Carrie thought about Bertie decorating a tree, carrying on with the celebrations of life in spite of the losses of three infant lives. Is that what you'd want me to do, Grandma?

She slid off the bed and dug in the bottom of the trunk, lifting out a small box. Opening it, she pulled out an object wrapped tightly in a yellowed handkerchief. Slowly, she unwound the wrappings, revealing a silver star. The one she and Grandma always put on top of the Christmas tree. She held it in her hands, remembering Grandma's words. "Like the Wise Men, always follow the star God puts in your sky."

I don't see any star in my sky.

"Maybe you're not looking for it." It wasn't an audible voice. Just the barest whisper of an idea.

Carrie wrinkled her forehead and stared at the star in her hand, turning it over, then turning it back. She walked to the dresser and leaned the silver ornament against the wall next to the picture of her and her grandmother. Might as well make a shrine of this. She took the locket from around her neck and set it next to the star.

Stepping back, she stood quietly, looking at the star, the photo, the locket. Symbols of the past. Remembrances of the people who birthed and nurtured her. What would they want for me now? Carrie knew the answer even as she asked it. They'd want her to embrace life. All of it. The good and the bad.

A calmness fell over her like big, soft snowflakes drifting toward earth on a winter evening.

"Merry Christmas," she whispered. "And peace on earth."

She slept hard that night, waking with a positive attitude toward a day that only last night promised to be difficult. Sifting through her wardrobe, she picked a turquoise shirtwaist to wear with a brown skirt. Brushing her hair, she pulled wispy curls toward her cheeks, then set a dark brown velvet hat on her head.

As he promised, James picked her up at noon. While driving up the long driveway to the Landon home, Carrie wondered how they'd all fit in the small house. The car had barely stopped when Jennie came running out the front door, squealing, "Merry Christmas, Miss Wyngate. I'm so glad you're here." She reached for Carrie's hand and pulled her teacher into the house.

It was all one large room, a small living room taking up the right half of the space and a kitchen taking up the left. In the middle, a hallway led to where Carrie supposed the bedrooms were located. Beyond the kitchen, the back door stood open onto a large, screened veranda where a long table and chairs were set up. Eating outside on Christmas Day was a thought that had never occurred to Carrie. Why not? It might be warm enough with sunlight flooding the back yard.

She was immediately drawn to it, but James was motioning toward an older couple seated at the kitchen table. "Carrie, these are my parents, Agnes and William Landon. Mom, Dad. Miss Carolyn Wyngate."

They greeted each other, and Carrie noticed the close resemblance between Mr. Landon and his sons. Mrs. Landon was a small woman with graying hair pulled into a bun on top of her head. She had brown eyes that looked exactly like Nate's. She wore a red dress with a large white apron.

Mrs. Landon was peeling potatoes ,and her husband was cracking nuts. James' wife, Helen, stood at the stove stirring something. Carrie asked what she could do and was assigned to set the table with Jennie's help. Walking out to the table on the veranda, she immediately saw there was a fireplace at one end of the porch with a fire burning brightly, making it comfortable for outdoor eating. As she and Jennie set the table, Jennie chattered non-stop about the new kittens in the woodshed, the Christmas gifts she received that morning and her baby brother who had been sick the day before. "But he's all better now," she added.

As they finished setting out the plates and cutlery, Carrie suggested they make a centerpiece for the table. Jennie clapped her hands, then asked ,"What will we use?"

"Let's take a walk and see if there are some flowers or plants that we can turn into a nice arrangement."

Jennie jumped from the veranda and skipped around the back yard. "We don't have any flowers this time of year."

Carrie pointed. "There's a bush with shiny, green leaves. We could cut a few branches of that. Let's see, what else could we use?" She looked around the yard but saw nothing. "Jennie, do you have any red paper?"

"Yes, Miss Wyngate. There's some left over from the paper chains we made for our Christmas tree."

"Good. Let's see if we can cut out some red paper leaves or flowers and intermingle them with the real leaves."

"Oh, that's a wonderful idea, Miss Wyngate!" Jennie darted into the house and came back with red paper and scissors. Together, she and Carrie cut out various red shapes and poked them among the green leaves.

Jennie clapped her hands. "That looks beautiful!"

Carrie and Jennie worked for half an hour, and when they finished, they stood back and admired the green and red arrangement on the middle of the table. It looked festive. Jennie was delighted and ran to each family member, pulling them to the table to see the Christmas decoration. They all declared it very creative.

Carrie returned to the kitchen and offered to stir the gravy. Within a short while, dinner preparations were complete, and the women carried the food to the table on the veranda. Carrie wondered where Nate was. Everyone was here. They were ready to sit down and eat. Where could he be? Perhaps he heard she was coming and absented himself. Had he connected with Mary? No. That couldn't be. Mary had gone to her parents' home in San Diego.

James took his place at the head of the table, his wife at the other end. Next to her sat the baby in his highchair. The elder Landons sat on one side with their grandson, Paul, between them.

Carrie was directed to the other side of the table in the middle. "I want to sit next to Miss Wyngate," Jennie said and sat down on Carrie's left between her teacher and her father. The chair to Carrie's right remained vacant.

James cleared his throat. "I don't know where Nate is. We don't want the food to get cold, so Dad, please have the blessing for us."

The "Amen" still floated in the air when the front door opened and Nate strode through the house and to the veranda. "Sorry to be late, everybody. Ran into our neighbor on my way over here. We started talking about Mr. Hatfield. Raymond has some interesting information about the man and his experiments."

Chapter Twenty-two

Nate took the empty seat next to Carrie and greeted her as he unfolded his napkin and spread it across his lap. He agreed to share what he'd learned from the neighbor only after they had finished eating. By then, a late afternoon breeze had come up, and they moved inside to eat dessert. They sat in the small living room holding plates of apple pie piled high with whipped cream.

"First of all," Nate began, "Charles Hatfield does not call himself a rain-maker. He says his work is a moisture or rain-enhancing endeavor. He's done a lot of study and research—"

"He's a scientist?" Mr. Landon interjected.

"Yes and no, Dad. He's a sewing machine salesman by trade. Studied and experimented for years on the subject of weather."

"A sewing machine salesman!" Nate's mother rolled her eyes as she spoke.

"Now, Mother. Let's not put a man down for being self-taught," Nate said. "His studies have led him to a method of releasing chemicals into the air. He does it from a tower."

"Chemicals. That's what he's going to use at Morena Reservoir?" James asked.

"Guess so."

"We ought to go up there and see him in action," James continued.

"I don't think so. According to our neighbor, Mr. Hatfield does not disclose his secrets. Neither does he want anyone observing him. One of his brothers always helps him."

The elder Mr. Landon set his fork on his plate. "I've always been wary of a man who is secretive. If he has bona fide methods that work, what's he got to hide?"

Nate lifted another forkful of pie toward his mouth, then set it down on the plate again. "Good point, Dad. On the other hand, he has some successes to his credit."

"It rained?" Nate's mother asked.

"Yes. In 1904 Hatfield set up a tower in the Los Angeles area. Next day it rained more than an inch. Came back in December the same year and produced more than nineteen inches of rain. In sixty days."

Mrs. Landon set her empty plate in her lap. "I don't think mortal men should go around bragging that they produced rain. God is in charge of the elements."

Everyone looked her way, nobody saying anything, until James finally said. "Mother, you know we all believe in God. We also believe in the scientific methods that He is probably ultimately in charge of. God can use human hands and minds to do His work."

Mrs. Landon eyed James and said, "We still ought to give God the credit."

A loud clanging, like a bell or metal striking metal, startled everyone. Carrie jumped to her feet. "What is that?"

Nate and James were already on their feet and halfway out the door. "Fire alarm," Nate hollered back over his shoulder. Within seconds, they were tearing out of the front yard in James' car.

The children ran to the window and watched the men leave. "I wonder where the fire is?" Jennie asked.

"It's so dry," Helen said. "It could spread quickly."

Mrs. Landon twisted her fingers together. "What a terrible time for a fire. On Christmas Day." Without changing her voice, she immediately started praying aloud. "God, get this fire under control quickly and take care of all those fighting it."

"Mommy, can we go outside and see if there's smoke in the sky?" Jennie had her hand on the door knob.

Nate's father rose to his feet. "I'm going out."

Within seconds they all stood in the yard, squinting in all directions. They saw nothing. Nate's father kept staring toward the southwest. "Maybe it's under control already."

"It's getting chilly out here," Helen said, "Come on, let's go back inside."

The family traipsed into the house but couldn't sit still. The children kept looking out the windows. The adults milled about as well. Helen said "I'm going to make a pot of coffee and some hot chocolate for the kids."

That calmed everyone and they gathered about the kitchen table. Helen set out a plate of Christmas cookies, and Carrie asked if she could help with the drinks.

As she stirred hot milk on the stove for the chocolate, the conversation buzzed about her, all of it centered on the fire. They hoped it wasn't anybody they knew; but in this community, everybody knew everybody. The biggest concern was the dry weather and the wind that had come up. A fire could skip from one roof to another. A spark could land in dry grass and poof! acres would be gone in minutes.

"Remember when the Herman Hotel burned down?" Mrs. Landon asked.

"Do I!" her husband responded. "That was a huge fire. They managed to keep it from spreading, though. Didn't harm the carriage house. It's still there."

Carrie listened quietly. She didn't have the history or connections in this town that the Landon family did. It was more personal for them, though she worried about James and Nate. Did volunteer firefighters have enough expertise to fight fires without endangering themselves unnecessarily? She had no idea but hoped they did.

They stayed at the table like pioneers who had circled the wagons during danger and talked about one thing after another. Every so often someone interjected "I hope the men will be back soon."

"I'm sure they will," Nate's father said. "If it had been a big fire, we would have seen smoke. Since we didn't see any smoke, my guess is that it's not big and they'll be back here before we know it." He sipped his coffee and reached for another cookie.

The sun slipped behind the lemon grove. Shadows filled the yard. It would be dark soon. Nate and James had not returned. Carrie lifted a cup of coffee to her mouth. It must be harder to fight a fire in the dark than in the daylight. Her fingertips felt cold. She curled them around her cup to warm them. The men had left without jackets. They must be cold. No, they'd be hot. How close do firefighters get to flames? Carrie shuddered.

Helen stood and announced that she needed to feed the baby. "Mind if I pull up his highchair and sit beside him so I can spoon some cereal into him?" The family scooted their chairs aside and made room for her.

Jennie and her brother played with their Christmas toys. Carrie noticed that Paul pushed a wooden car around the room, while Jennie laid a doll in a new-looking wooden cradle. Both objects looked very well made and Carrie figured their father must have made them. She had no sooner thought it than Jennie came to her and said "Miss Wyngate, come and see the nice cradle Uncle Nate made for me for Christmas."

Carrie followed the girl and knelt on the rug beside her to examine the cradle. It was beautifully made, the finish smooth and satiny when she rubbed her hand across it. "Your uncle is a real craftsman."

"Uncle Nate is nice."

A noise outside alerted everyone in the room. The children ran to the window. "They're back!" they yelled.

James' wife was already opening the door. Outside, Carrie could hear stomping of feet as Nate and James clumped across the porch. "We're taking our shoes off outside," James said. "We're pretty dirty."

Helen stepped outside and into her husband's arms. "I don't care if you're dirty. I'm so glad you're here."

Both men walked in, their faces sooty, their clothes grimy and smelling of smoke. Their family surrounded them immediately, while Carrie hung back. Over everyone's head, she saw Nate look her direction. For some reason, tears came to her eyes. She blinked them back as she smiled at Nate.

"Where was the fire?" Nate's father asked.

Nate rubbed his hands together as if to remove the soot. "You won't believe this, but it was the Owenses' home."

Carrie's hand flew to her mouth. "Oh, no!"

Nate pulled himself away from his family and moved toward her. Carrie looked into his eyes. "What happened?"

"Mrs. Owens left a roasting pan on the stove," Nate began. "It had grease in it. She forgot to turn off the stove. They fell asleep in the living room. The smoke and odor awoke them. Mr. Owens threw salt on the flames which subdued it somewhat. Still, flames were leaping up the wall behind the stove when we got there."

"Much damage?" Nate's father asked.

"The wall is charred pretty bad," James said. "Some of the flames reached the ceiling and burned it. There's smoke damage."

"Are Mr. and Mrs. Owens alright?" Carrie asked, trying to control the quaver in her voice.

Nate looked at her. "They're shaken up, but they'll be alright."

Carrie took a step away from Nate. "I must go to them."

Nate pulled her back. "Wait a minute. You need to know about the rest of the house."

Suddenly, Carrie remembered her bedroom was directly above the kitchen. "Oh, my room. Is it damaged?"

"Yes and no," Nate replied. "We didn't know how far the flames from below had burned, so we had to chop into the wall and flooring of your room. You have a hole in your floor, but we covered it up with a rug." He grinned and she glared at him.

"That's not funny!"

Nate stopped grinning and said, "Everything else in your room is as it was. Right down to the shawl lying across your bed."

Carrie let out a long sigh. "Good, but of course, people are more important than my things. That's why I want to get back to the Owenses' as quickly as possible."

"Afraid that's not a good idea, Carrie."

"Why not?"

"Remember, there's a hole in your floor. And the room smells smoky. You shouldn't sleep there tonight. The Owenses are taking a room at the hotel for a night or two."

"Where am I going to go?" Carrie tried to keep the panic out of her voice.

"We've got an extra room," Nate's mother said. "You're most welcome to spend the night with us."

Carrie looked at her, then Mr. Landon. They smiled. Finally, she glanced at Nate, whose face had taken on a detached look like a hotel clerk checking in one of many guests for the night.

Chapter Twenty-three

When Nate and Carrie and his parents arrived at their home, it was cold. Nate quickly got a fire going in the fireplace, and the four of them drew up chairs near the heat.

"Kind of chilly this evening," Mr. Landon said. "How is it in Chicago this time of year, Carrie?"

"Very cold and usually some snow. I think I'm going to like the winters here much better."

They all laughed.

"It's easy to like Chula Vista," Mr. Landon continued. "The weather. The opportunity to own a piece of land. The ocean nearby. The mountains not too far away."

"The only downside," Mrs Landon interrupted, "is that we need rain."

"After talking with our neighbor," Nate said, "I think that Mr. Charles Hatfield might be able to help us with that. To me, it's sounding more and more like there might be scientific principles behind what he is doing."

Nate's mother frowned. "Now, Nate. Don't go putting your faith in some man, instead of God."

"Mother, I didn't say that. I don't think science and God are opposing forces." Nate wrinkled his forehead and stared into the fire. "I'm not throwing away my faith," he said quietly.

His mother didn't answer, and Carrie felt relieved that this brief skirmish had ended. Before long, Mr. Landon stood and said "It's time for me to go to bed. Are you coming along too, Mother?"

Mrs. Landon stood. "First, let me show Carrie her room."

"I'll do that," Nate said almost too quickly.

Minutes later, he led Carrie up the stairs and to a room at the end of a hall. He opened the door, and moonlight streamed through the window, creating a silvery path on the floor and across the bed. Carrie caught her breath and moved toward the window. Nate followed and stood beside her.

"It's pretty, isn't it?" he said, "Even if it's not quite a full moon."

"I always leave the curtains open to let in sunlight and moonlight. It's so quiet and peaceful here. We never had views like this in Chicago. Our windows only looked out on other buildings and rooftops."

Nate glanced at Carrie. "Then you like it here...in Chula Vista?"

"I'm beginning to feel at home. The Owenses are very good to me. I want to help them get their house back in order. Tomorrow, can you take me there so I can start cleaning?"

"I was thinking the same thing...that I'd like to help fix their house."

Carrie turned to him. "Let's go first thing in the morning."

"There's one problem." Nate looked beyond Carrie, then back at her. "Tomorrow's church day for most people around here. Neighbors might not like us banging around in there. Hardware store and lumber yard will be closed, too. I won't be able to buy any supplies if I need them."

"The only supplies I need are soap and water."

Nate turned toward the window again. "Tell you what, Carrie, if you'll go to church with me—with us—in the morning, we'll go over there in the afternoon and see what we can do."

"You forget that I don't have my church clothes with me." To herself, she thought about the fact that she had no sleeping clothes with her, either. Or toothbrush. Or hairbrush. She felt unkempt with no possibility of remedying the situation.

"I'll take you to the Owenses' house first thing in the morning, right after breakfast, so you can get a change of clothes, your personal items, whatever you need."

"Thank you, Nate. I really appreciate that." She stepped away from the window and set her purse down on a chest of drawers.

Nate stood awkwardly for a minute, then walked out the door saying, "Good night, Carrie. If you need anything, I'll be in the next room down the hall." He shut the door quietly behind him.

Carrie took off her skirt and shirtwaist and hung them on a peg on the wall. She pulled back the bedcovers and slipped under them, wearing her undergarments. It didn't feel comfortable. She wished she had her night-gown. What would she do in the morning to make herself look and feel presentable? She tried placing her head on the pillow in a way that wouldn't muss her hair too much and fell into thoughts of Nate in the next room.

The idea made her whole body tingle. He had said, "If you need any-thing..." Standing next to him at the window had rattled her resolve about not needing anything from any man.

The moonlight must have affected her. Carrie stared at the ceiling a long time, then finally squeezed her eyes shut to blot out the moonlight, but the appealing picture of Nate wouldn't go away.

Nate couldn't go to sleep. He kept thinking of Carrie. It had seemed so right to have her with him and his family all day, not that it had been any of his doing. He knew the rule James lived by: to make sure no teacher was left alone on a holiday; still, he wondered if his brother had a deeper reason for inviting Carrie to be with them.

There would be tomorrow with her, too. The fire in the Owenses' kitchen had turned into a blessing for him. He'd work his heart out helping Carrie repair their property. Undoubtedly, it would take more than a day to get the house back into shape. He didn't care how many days it took. Nothing could be better than extended time with Carrie, unless he messed it up. He hoped he wouldn't.

She was so pretty standing by the window in the moonlight. Knowing she slept in the next room, set his heart pounding. He meant what he said: "If you need anything." He wondered if she would ever need him like he was beginning to feel he needed her. It made him shiver, and he flung his body first one direction and then the other, trying to find a comfortable spot in the bed. Finally, the exertion of fighting a fire overtook him, and he fell asleep, not to waken until morning.

Carrie rose early and was standing at the kitchen sink drinking a glass of water when Nate came downstairs and entered the room. She heard him and turned, flinging her hands to her head in a futile gesture to hide her hair.

"Your hair looks beautiful," he said.

"You're teasing me. It's a mess, and I'm not in the habit of greeting the world with uncombed hair."

"I'm not teasing." Nate turned toward the refrigerator and withdrew a basket of eggs. "I'm pretty good at scrambling eggs. Why don't I make us a little breakfast and we can be on our way to the Owenses' house."

"Sounds good. Let me help."

Nate had his head in the refrigerator again. "How about some chopped onions in those eggs? And here's some leftover sandwich meat I can slice and add." He pointed to a loaf of homemade bread on the counter. "Could you slice some bread and make the toast?"

"Be happy to."

Within a short while, breakfast was on the table, and they sat across from each other eating. When they finished, they stacked the dirty dishes in the sink, slipped on jackets and left the house before Mr. and Mrs. Landon got up.

As she sat in the truck, Carrie crossed her arms with her hands tucked under her armpits. "It's cool this morning."

"Maybe that's because it's only eight in the morning and the sun has only been up an hour." He looked at Carrie and smiled. "I'm generally not up very early on a Sunday."

It didn't take long to drive to the Owenses' house. Nate parked the truck in front, and they walked up to the door. He reached in his pocket. "Mr. Owens gave me a key to the house yesterday."

He unlocked the door, held it for Carrie to enter and followed her in. The house smelled like damp soot. Carrie coughed. "Let's open all the windows and start airing the place out."

The living room looked normal, but when they walked into the kitchen, Carrie gasped. The whole wall behind the stove was burned. Jagged holes in the plaster exposed the studs beneath. Gray streaks ran a third of the way across the ceiling. The floor was wet with sooty water from the firefighters' work. Carrie tiptoed through it toward the sink, which was filled with dirty dishes. The windows were fogged over with smoke, as were the cabinets and countertops. She ran a finger over the table, which came up covered in black grime.

"Everything's going to have to be scrubbed."

"Looks like it," Nate said as he reached toward the burned wall and began tearing into it with the hammer he'd brought from his truck. "This whole wall needs to be removed before we can put up a new one." He threw a chunk of blackened plaster onto the floor. "Why don't you change into your church clothes? We'll go back to the house, pick up the folks, go to church. Then we'll come back here after lunch and start work."

"Oh, I wish we could start now. There's so much to do."

"With both of us working on it, we'll get a lot done this afternoon."

"I hope so because this looks awful."

Carrie dismissed herself and climbed the stairs to change clothes, wash her face and fix her hair. When she returned, Nate had piled chunks of blackened plaster in the middle of the floor..

"Looks like you've been busy."

He grinned at her. "I've never been good at standing around doing nothing. Now look at me. I'm going to have to clean up and change clothes before church."

News of the fire spread throughout the community. By the time Nate and Carrie arrived at church, a group of people had surrounded the Owenses inquiring on how they were doing. Since Nate had been at the fire scene, people talked with him, too.

On the drive home after the services, Nate reported that half a dozen folk had volunteered to help clean the Owenses' home that afternoon. "Several more said they'd help in the next few days, too."

Carrie clapped her hands together. "How wonderful, Nate!"

"Folks around here like to help each other."

Chapter Twenty-four

As soon as they finished eating the Sunday meal that Mrs. Landon had cooked, Nate and Carrie drove to the Owenses' house. Nate immediately started tearing out more of the burned wall behind the stove while Carrie filled a bucket with water and soap and began scrubbing walls in the living room. About that time, Mr. and Mrs. Owens arrived. As soon as Bertie walked into the kitchen, she started crying. Her husband took her in his arms. "I know it looks bad in here, Bertie, but it can all be repaired. The important thing is that we were not injured."

Nate stopped what he was doing long enough to say, "We've got a work bee coming in a few moments. Why don't you folk relax a bit, take a walk or something while we get started?"

Carrie hurried toward the Owenses and threw her arms around Bertie. "Don't you worry about anything. Nate and I and the others will get this all cleaned up. The men will fix the wall. It'll be better than new."

Bertie lifted her head from her husband's chest. "That's so wonderful of you, but we can't sit around and let other people do all the work."

"Why can't you?" Carrie asked. "You've had a very upsetting thing happen. I know you'd be quick to help someone in this situation. You relax and let others help you."

Mr. Owens grinned at Carrie. "It sounds like you're running us out of here."

Carrie laughed. "I guess I am."

"I am, too," Nate said.

Mr. Owens steered his wife into the living room and out the front door. On their way out, they passed Mike, the owner of the lumber yard, and his friend, Albert, who owned a packing plant. "We're here to help," they said and the Owenses thanked them profusely.

When Mike saw the damaged wall in the kitchen, he immediately began calculating what they'd need to fix it. "I think we ought to replace parts of some of those studs. I've got plenty of two by fours over at the shop. I'll unlock the place and we'll go round to the back and get it. I'll contact Shafer, too, because we'll need plaster and nails. I know he'll be glad to help. We work together pretty well."

Carrie returned to the living room just as a whole family walked through the open front door. "Hello! We're here to go to work." A tall, skinny man with a plump wife and two lanky teen-aged sons stood on the doorstep. Carrie invited them in, and soon they had put themselves to the task of carrying the ash-covered Christmas tree out to the front yard, where they dismantled it. The woman dusted and cleaned the ornaments, placing them carefully in the storage boxes.

"I'm taking Mike in my truck to get some lumber for the kitchen and the upstairs bedroom." Nate announced to Carrie on his way out.

The two men drove away, returning less than an hour later with boards and other supplies. Everyone stopped what they were doing and helped carry the items into the kitchen. As the men began working, Carrie suggested that she and the woman and her sons vacate the room to give the men more room to work.

"I started cleaning the walls in the living room. Could you help me with that?" she asked. The boys disappeared for several minutes, then reappeared with two ladders, which they climbed on to reach the ceiling and upper parts of the walls. After they finished that task, they carried the upholstered furniture to the front yard and brushed it.

The sounds of sawing emanated from the back porch. The noise of hammers filled the kitchen. No one heard or saw the minister enter the house. He stood in the middle of the kitchen, dressed in a red-checked shirt and blue overalls. Finally, one of the men noticed him. "Hello, Reverend. We know this isn't the usual way to honor the Lord's Day...."

"It seems quite appropriate," the minister said. "I came by to see if you needed another pair of hands."

"Thanks, Reverend," Nate said, "Could you come tomorrow? We're about to finish for today. These winter days are too short."

"Be glad to come back tomorrow. Let me help you put your tools and things away."

While people cleaned up the work area, Carrie stole upstairs to her room. She looked at the jagged holes in the floor and the wall, then gathered some clothes and personal items into a large tapestry bag and returned downstairs. Nate was standing at the front door, thanking everyone as they left. He turned toward her, his face sweaty and lined with black streaks.

Carrie laughed. "You look like a clown!"

He grimaced at her. "Is that better?"

"Much better." Out of nowhere, the idea came to her that it would be impossible for Nate not to look good to her. Carrie quickly stuffed those thoughts in the bottom drawer of her mind.

Nate held the door open for her. "Let's go home. I'm sure Mom will have some food for us."

As they drove, Nate mulled over the word "us." He liked it, and he liked the comfortable way he had felt all day working alongside Carrie.

"A penny for your thoughts," Carrie said.

"I was thinking about what a nice day this has been."

"Tearing up a wall in a smoky-smelling kitchen is what you consider nice?"

"Definitely. I like to create beauty out of disaster."

"You're sounding poetic, Nate." Carrie laughed, and it sent goose bumps up his spine.

"I'm not a poet. Just a guy who likes to make things with his hands."

"Jennie told me you made the doll cradle for her and the car for her brother. You do beautiful work."

"Thanks, Carrie." Her compliment made him feel like he could conquer anything he set his mind to. Every minute with Carrie confirmed that she was what he had his mind and heart set on. The question begging an answer was how to bring her to feel the same about him.

Carrie sat with the Landon family that evening before the fire. Nate talked about the work of the day, and his father offered a suggestion or two on repairing the kitchen wall. The warmth from the fireplace made Carrie drowsy, and she excused herself early to go to bed. Before she fell asleep, she thought about the next day and hoped they could finish their work at the Owenses' house. Though she had to admit that she enjoyed working on the house with Nate, she wanted to be back in her own room in her own bed.

She slept hard and long. A knock on her door and a voice calling, "Carrie, wake up!" jolted her upright. Why was Nate calling her? She looked at the window. The sun was up. She rubbed her eyes, swung her legs out of bed and gradually stood. Wrapping a robe about her, she opened the door a crack. Nate stood there, energetic, smiling, ready to start the day.

"I'll be ready in a few minutes," she said and closed the door on his eager face. Fifteen minutes later, she descended the stairs and entered the kitchen, where Nate's mother was serving breakfast. Nate and his father sat at the table drinking cups of coffee. They invited her to join them.

Nate said he was anxious to get to work on the Owenses' house, so they hurried through breakfast and left immediately. Once they let themselves into the house, they set to work where they had left off the day before. Within two hours, all the helpers from the previous day had arrived. By mid-afternoon, the kitchen had a new wall, though the fresh plaster was still wet. Walls, floors and counter tops had all been washed, as well as walls in other rooms.

"I'd like to get the hole in the floor and wall upstairs repaired today," Nate said as he headed for the stairs. Carrie followed him. It seemed odd for the two of them to be standing in her bedroom. Nate was all business, assessing the damage, figuring out how to fix it. He enlisted the minister's help, and within a couple of hours, the job was finished.

"Oh, good! I can sleep here tonight!" Carrie said.

Nate looked at her with serious eyes. "I'd rather you didn't."

"Why not?"

"There's still the smell of smoke in the air, and—"

"And what?"

"I'd worry about you being here all alone."

"You think I've never been alone?"

"No, I don't think that at all. It's just that...that...." Nate searched for words. "I'd feel better if you were with me...at our house...at least one more night." His eyes studied her.

"Look, Nate, I really appreciate your hospitality, and your family has been very kind to me...."

"It's settled then," he said with finality in his voice. "You'll stay with us one more night."

Carrie shrugged her shoulders. "Oh, alright. One more night, but that's it. I don't want to burden you or your parents."

"You're not a burden, Carrie. You're an asset...to me." He stepped closer and looked into her eyes. "A very beautiful asset, too." He leaned his face toward hers, but she stepped back and looked away from him.

They said little to each other as they drove to Nate's home. Carrie couldn't believe she had rejected a kiss from Nate Landon. He was everything she'd want in a man. Good looking. Kind. Hard working. Talented.

The thing that troubled her was that she didn't know if she was ready for a man in her life. Would she ever be? What if she lost her chance with him? Mary would snatch him up. She was certain of that. Carrie felt panic rise in her chest. How could she undo the damage she'd done?

Carrie looked over at Nate. He kept his eyes straight ahead on the road. "Nate, I'm sorry about...about...turning away from you."

She watched the muscles working in his jaw. He still didn't look her direction, and he didn't say anything until he parked the truck in front of the Landon home. Then he turned to her. "I really care about you, Carrie. I was hoping you might feel the same toward me. Apparently, you don't."

"I'm not sure what I care about," she said in a small voice.

"Well, if you're not sure, I'll back off." He opened the door of the truck and started to get out. "Let me know if you ever become sure."

He walked around the car, opened the door for her and walked beside her to the front door. They both put on happy faces to greet Nate's parents.

Chapter Twenty-five

Most the next day, Carrie and Nate avoided each other, even though they both worked at the Owenses' house. Nate painted the kitchen and bedroom walls while Carrie continued scrubbing every inch of the house.

Late in the day, the Owenses returned to their home. That night, Carrie slept in her own room. Wednesday morning, Bertie flung open all the doors and windows to air the rooms of their smoky scent. Though the sun was shining, the air felt cool. Carrie wore a sweater as she helped with more clean-up chores. Bertie was determined to wash all the curtains and bedding in the house to remove all traces of smoke.

Carrie was glad to be busy. It took her mind away from Nate. Late in the afternoon, she decided to take a walk and headed down the street past the Congregational Church. The minister was just coming out, saw her and called out a greeting. Carrie walked toward him and thanked him for his help with the cleanup of the Owenses' home.

"Glad I could help. That Nate Landon is quite the worker and organizer. It's amazing how he pulled everybody together and we got so much accomplished."

"Yes. That was quite a crew," Carrie responded, trying not to let her face reveal the commotion in her heart at the mention of Nate.

"The church is having a New Year's Eve service this Friday evening at 8 p.m., followed with a social hour. I'd like to invite you to come. And would you remind the Owens' about it?"

"Thank you, Reverend. I'll tell them." Carrie didn't want to promise to attend, so she excused herself and continued her walk. A small dog came out of nowhere and started following her. "You don't want to hang around me," she said to the animal, "if you're looking for permanent friendship."

The dog cocked his head and trotted to her side.

"You're a persistent one," she said, "Like someone else I know."

The dog stayed with her until it spied some children playing in a yard and ran to them. Carrie was relieved and kept walking. She hadn't gone far when a car roared down the street and stopped abruptly at a nearby house. She watched as a man and woman leaped out, opened the back door of the car, and lifted a child from the seat and hurried to the house where they knocked loudly. Carrie drew closer. The door of the house opened and she heard the couple with the child ask "Is the doctor in?"

They entered the house, and the door shut, leaving Carrie to wonder who the child was and what was wrong. She hadn't recognized the couple or the car. As she continued her walk, she found herself whispering, "God, please take care of that child." What if it were one of her students? It didn't matter. Any child in trouble always stirred Carrie.

She told the Owenses about the incident, and they assured her that the doctor who lived in that house was a very competent person. "We'll probably hear all about it tomorrow," Mr. Owens said.

The next morning, news had spread around town that a Japanese boy had fallen out of a tree and broken his arm. His parents didn't have a car, so neighbors brought the boy to the doctor.

"I hope it wasn't David," Carrie immediately said, "How can I find out who it was?"

"You could talk with Mr. Rising, who publishes our weekly newspaper."

Carrie lost no time in going to town and finding the Chula Vista Review office on the east side of Third Avenue. Mr. Rising looked up from a pile of papers and said, "I was just out there at the parents' home trying to get the story. Pretty hard to do, when they speak only Japanese. It was the boy, himself, who told me about his accident. His name was...let me see...I wrote it down here somewhere. Imamura. David Imamura. Smart kid. Spoke flawless English."

Carrie gasped. "He's one of my students. Can you tell me how to get to his home?"

"It's quite a ways. Northeast part of town.... Here, I'll draw a map."

Carrie took the map and studied it. It's not too far to walk, is it?"

Mr. Rising looked at Carrie's feet and said, "Depends on what kind of shoes you're wearing."

"I've got better walking shoes. I'm going right home to put them on.

Thank you, Mr. Rising, for the information."

As soon as Carrie changed into sturdier shoes, she set out for the Imamura place, following the map she held in her hands. She must have walked half the distance when the thought occurred to her that the Imamuras might not welcome her into their home. She stopped for a second, then stepped forward again. I've come this far. I'm not turning back now.

The road bent and beyond that, Carrie saw a house sitting on the side of a hill. Surrounding it, the hill had been terraced and planted with rows of vegetables and small fruit trees. The house was small, and two children sat on the front step, one of them with his arm in a white sling. He saw her, jumped down and ran toward her, followed by another boy—Charlie Jenkins.

"Miss Wyngate," both boys called as they charged toward her.

"David, Charlie, slow down or you'll fall." Carrie spread her arms to catch both of them. They stopped inches from her, panting.

"I broke my arm," David said as he held it up for her inspection.

"So I heard. That's why I came out to see how you are doing."

"You walked all the way out here by yourself, Miss Wyngate, just to see me?"

"I sure did."

"Wow! I'm going to tell my parents to come out." David turned and ran back to the house, leaving Carrie and Charlie standing next to a row of lettuce.

"You came out here, too, Charlie, to see David."

"He's my friend. I rode my bike."

"That's thoughtful of you, Charlie."

A few minutes later, David returned with his parents in tow and two younger siblings. They bowed to Carrie, and she bowed in return. David translated for them. "We are much honored that you came to see our son."

"I was worried about him."

"Thank you for your worry," is what they said back, via David's translation.

Carrie faced David. "It's your right arm that's broken. That's going to make it hard for you to write."

"Teacher, I'm going to help him with his schoolwork." Charlie beamed at her, then David.

"Splendid, Charlie. We'll put your desks together so it will be easy for you to help him."

As soon as she said those words, Carrie wondered what Mr. Jenkins would think of such an unorthodox arrangement in the classroom. She shut it out of her mind and asked David how long he would be wearing a cast.

"Six weeks."

"That'll go by fast. I'm glad you've got a friend like Charlie to help you."

"I'm going to help him with the gardening, too," Charlie announced.

"Do your parents know about this?"

"They know I came to see David today. I'm sure they won't mind if I come back and help him. At least, Mom won't mind." Charlie scrunched his toe in the dirt.

After a few more minutes of visiting, Carrie said goodbye, and the two boys walked with her down the slope toward the main road. "I'll see both you boys next Monday," Carrie said.

"I'm glad school is starting again," David said. "I got kind of bored during the vacation."

"Is that why you were climbing a tree?"

David grinned. "Maybe. Anyway, Miss Wyngate, I'll see you Monday."

"See you," Charlie echoed.

"You probably shouldn't stay out here too late, Charlie," Carrie said. "It gets dark early during winter and your parents will worry about you."

"I'm leaving pretty soon, Miss Wyngate. I can go pretty fast on my bicycle."

As she walked home, Carrie mused over the two boys and their unlikely friendship. Goes to show you, she told herself, that you never know where friendship will blossom. Her heart told her to apply those thoughts to her friendship with Nate. If it were a friendship.

When she arrived at home, Bertie set her down at the kitchen table, put a cup of hot coffee in her hands and wanted to know all about her trip to the Imamuras. "What was their house like?"

"I didn't go inside," Carrie said as she stirred her coffee. "Halfway out there, I thought I might be making a tremendous social gaffe by visiting them. It worked itself out. We stood outside and visited."

"Oh." Bertie sounded disappointed that Carrie didn't have startling revelations to share. "I know they're people, like all people, but I've always felt the races shouldn't mingle."

"What do you mean by that?" Carrie asked.

"They're so different. It's better they stay to themselves and we stay to ourselves. We definitely wouldn't want any inter-marriage."

"Hm-m-m-m," Carrie said and decided to change the subject to something else. "Bertie, I've been thinking I'd like to go to National City tomorrow—actually out to Paradise Valley Sanitarium. The train can get me there, can't it?"

"Yes. When you get off at the station in National City, ask for directions to the sanitarium. Why do you want to go there?"

"Someone told me they had a well of water that's the result of a miracle."

"That's true. I've heard of it."

"I'd like to see a water miracle. Maybe it would help me get more excited about Mr. Hatfield sending chemicals up in the air to petition the gods for rain."

Bertie laughed, which relieved Carrie to know that her remarks hadn't been taken as too irreligious by the older woman.

Chapter Twenty-six

Carrie felt a little foolish the next morning embarking on a journey to view a water well. The trip took a couple of hours, but when she arrived at the Paradise Valley Sanitarium property, she was overwhelmed with the lush grounds. Plants, trees and flowers grew everywhere. There seemed to be no drought here. No wilted or dying vegetation. She inquired about the well, and a groundskeeper escorted her to the spot marked with a plaque. Carrie read the brief account of what she had heard earlier. Mr. Salem Hamilton dug to eighty-five feet before he struck a vein of water as large as a man's arm. It filled the well so rapidly that the workers had to abandon their tools and flee.

"Ten years later, this well is still providing all our water needs," the groundskeeper explained. "For the buildings and all these plants and trees."

Carrie shook her head. "I don't believe it."

"It's a miracle," the man said.

As she surveyed the area, Carrie thought about the city of San Diego hiring a rainmaker for the current water shortage. Would he perform a miracle or a scientific demonstration? Or fool everyone and run off with a pocketful of money? What did it matter, as long as it rained?

In her heart, Carrie felt that it mattered, but it was hard to know what to believe. She thanked the gardener, wandered around the grounds a few more minutes, then stepped inside a building.

Sunlight streamed in through the windows of a large reception area, making the floors glisten like they had just been waxed. A lady at a desk smiled and asked, "May I help you?"

"I'm new to the area. Heard about this place and decided to see it for myself."

"Welcome!" The woman picked up a brochure and handed it to Carrie. "Here's some literature that describes our services. Actually, we like to consider ourselves in the ministry. Of healing."

"That's a different way of looking at it."

She and the receptionist talked a little longer. When she turned to leave, Carrie remarked "If I'm ever sick, I want to come here."

The woman smiled. "Hope you never are; but if you need us, we'll be here."

On the return trip to Chula Vista, Carrie leaned her head back, closed her eyes and let her mind replay the pictures of the miracle well, the beautiful grounds and the well-kept buildings. She thought how productive the land of Southern California could be. Add water and it blooms. Take away water and it dies. Everything depended on water.

Before she knew it, the train had returned to the small station on Third Avenue. She stepped down and came face to face with Nate. He looked as surprised to see her as she was to see him. Simultaneously, they both asked, "What are you doing here?"

Carrie told of her trip to see the miracle well. Nate said, "I'm here to see if there are any packages to deliver. I could give you a ride home."

"Thank you. I'd appreciate that."

Nate drove her from the station and toward the Owenses' home, where he parked in front of the house only long enough to open the door for her and escort her to the front door.

Inside the house, Bertie was setting the table for supper. Mr. Owens was reading the evening paper. "It says in the paper that Mr. Hatfield and his younger brother, Joel, will begin work at Morena Reservoir the first of January, 1916." He lowered the paper and looked at Carrie. "Good evening and welcome to the new year of rain."

Carrie chuckled. "How soon should I get out my umbrella?"

He grinned back at her. "That remains to be seen."

"Come to dinner," Bertie called.

While they ate, Carrie described her trip to the Paradise Valley Sanitarium and the miracle well, ending with a personal disclaimer that she wasn't sure if it were a miracle or a natural phenomenon.

"Which reminds me," Bertie said, "about the New Year's Eve service at the church this evening. You're coming, aren't you, Carrie? I always say church is the best place to start a new year."

Mr. Owens glanced at Carrie, then at his wife. "I know how much the church means to you, Honey, but maybe Carrie has other plans for this evening."

Carrie felt grateful for Mr. Owens' understanding, but his statement also produced a moral dilemma. She couldn't lie about "other plans" that she didn't have. In a town as small as Chula Vista, what else would there be to do?

"Of course I'm going." Carrie's words surprised herself.

The church service didn't surprise her. They sang a few hymns, listened to a short message by the reverend, had a prayer and dismissed to an adjacent social hall for coffee and cake. Carrie looked about the room and saw only two other young people, a young man and woman standing awkwardly against the wall. She approached them, introduced herself and they greeted her and quickly informed her that they were positive more young people would be coming later. "The old folks go home pretty soon and go to bed. All except for the chaperones," the young man said as he nodded toward an older couple sitting at a small table playing checkers. "We stay up till midnight to usher in the New Year. You'll stay, won't you?"

Carrie shrugged. "Why not? I'm too young to go to bed this early."

True to her new friends' prediction, the older adults began leaving, and one by one, younger people arrived. They all looked to be of high school age. When some of them learned she was a school teacher, that separated her from them even further. Carrie was not in the habit of giving up on projects she started, so she stayed. She did her best to join in their table games and conversations.

At 11:45, the door opened and Mary, Miguel and Nate walked in. It stunned her and she immediately tried to think of ways of exiting. Miguel walked toward a huge upright piano at the far end of the hall, saying. "We've got to have music to bring in the new year." He pulled out the bench, sat down and began pounding out ragtime music on the keys. Everyone crowded around him while keeping an eye on the clock on the opposite wall. One of the high schoolers passed out noisemakers. "Let's make a racket at midnight," he said. "I'd rather kiss a pretty girl at midnight," another boy said.

Carrie tried to wiggle her way out of the group. The countdown began. The young people's voices shouted "five...four...three...two...one...Happy New Year!" Miguel switched into playing "Auld Lang Syne," and a high school boy kissed Carrie on the lips. He passed her to another boy, but she dodged him. Suddenly, Miguel stopped playing the piano, leaped toward Carrie and bent to kiss her. She turned her face and his kiss landed on her cheek. As she escaped Miguel, she got a glimpse of Mary and Nate. Had they? Or hadn't they? They stood face to face, but Carrie couldn't see what they were doing. Too many bodies moved and squirmed about her. As fast as possible, she worked her way to the edge of the group, walked across the room and out the door.

Her face felt hot. She stopped a moment to pull out a handkerchief and blot the sweat from her forehead. The cold night air felt good. Hearing the door opening behind her, she walked briskly away. What if Miguel followed her? Or one of those high school boys? She was sure Nate wouldn't be tailing her. She'd feel safer if he did. She pulled her shawl tighter around her shoulders and picked up her pace. The footsteps behind sounded like they'd turned another direction. Carrie slowed and looked up at the black sky glistening with stars. Her grandmother's voice whispered in her head. Follow your star.

Blinking back tears, Carrie whispered, "I'm trying to, Grandma, but I don't know where it is."

Chapter Twenty-seven

On New Years Day, 1916, Nate and his brother, James, drove fifty miles toward the Morena Reservoir, then walked the last few miles. According to the newspaper, Charles Hatfield and his brother, Joel, had begun constructing their "moisture-enhancing" tower.

Charles stood high on a ladder, while Joel stood below, hoisting lumber to his older brother. Nate and James greeted both men. Charles said nothing. Joel grunted and asked, "What do you fellows want?"

"I'm James Landon and this is my brother, Nate. We live in Chula Vista and wanted to see for ourselves this rain-making project."

"My brother, Charles, does not claim to make rain. All he does is take advantage of existing conditions to enhance the moisture that is already in the air."

"How do you go about enhancing moisture?" Nate asked.

"Charles does not divulge any of his methods. All I can tell you is that he has been successful in the past. He'll be successful again."

"I hope so because our orchards and fields certainly need rain," James said.

"My brother is very sympathetic to the plight of farmers in this country. That's why he continues his work despite the ridicule he gets. Now, if you'll excuse us, we've got work to do."

Joel turned his back on Nate and James, who stood there for a few more minutes before turning and walking back down the trail.

"They weren't very friendly," Nate said. "It's like the reports we heard. Those men don't disclose anything."

"No, but I'm glad we came," James replied. "At least we saw a bit of history in the making."

"I wonder what kind of history it will be?" Nate slowed to pick his way through a rocky stretch of the trail. "Will we be laughing with Mr. Hatfield or at him?"

That evening, Nate and James described their encounter with the Hatfield brothers to their families. "All that way for nothing!" Nate's mother said.

Nate smiled at her. "At least I have something to report to the City Council."

"A report that will take less than a minute," James said, which made everyone laugh.

Carrie arrived early at school on Monday to move Charlie's desk next to David's. She hoped the arrangement would work well for both boys and not cause conflict with the other students, who might see this as favoritism. Another worry that sprang to mind was what Mr. Jenkins might think of her action. She decided to put both concerns out of her thoughts and focus on how to help Charlie help David.

The pupils bounced into the classroom like jumping beans in their eagerness to tell their teacher about their various experiences over the Christmas holiday. Carrie maintained order by promising that each student would be given an opportunity at the end of the day to share "my favorite thing about Christmas."

They settled down and bent their heads over their books. The last hour of the day was devoted to the children's stories. They took turns coming to the front and facing the classroom to give their speeches. Carrie surprised them by announcing that each of them would be given five points credit in elocution for their efforts. They skipped out of the classroom with happy faces.

Carrie took a deep breath. It had been a tiring day trying to recapture the children's interest in academic matters. She sat at her desk rubbing her temples with her fingers. The door opened and she looked up. It was Mary.

"Hello, Carrie."

"Hello, Mary. How did it go for you today?"

Mary walked toward her, saying "The children were pretty wiggly after being on vacation."

"Same here." Carrie couldn't think how to continue the conversation, and silence filled the space between them.

Mary looked around the room, then brought her eyes back to Carrie.

"You disappeared rather quickly after the New Year's Eve party."

Carrie shrugged. "You came late. I left early. What else is there to do once you've brought in the New Year?"

"Oh, plenty!" Mary's eyes grew excited.

Carrie didn't want to know what Mary had done after the party, so she started putting papers and pencils in the drawers of her desk. Mary took the hint and said, "I see you're busy, so I'll run along. Maybe we can get together some other time."

"That would be nice. Let's stay in touch."

Mid-morning on Wednesday, Jennie raised her hand.

"Yes, Jennie."

"Teacher. It's starting to rain."

All heads turned to the window. Gray clouds covered the sky, like they had since sunrise. At first, Carrie could see nothing different about the weather. Then, she saw a few sprinkles splat against the dirt.

Her students rose from their seats and moved to the window. "Boys and girls, please take your seats. We can all see better if we stay seated right where we are."

They sat down but kept their eyes on the window. "The rainmaker is making it rain!" one student said.

"Nah! He's a fake," someone else said.

"It's raining just because it wanted to," another child said.

"Please, children, raise your hands if you wish to speak."

Hands waved like flags before Carrie's eyes, and she decided to let them talk in an orderly way about what everyone in the community had been thinking and talking about for weeks. Perhaps, out of the discussion, she could help them learn to think logically and express themselves clearly.

"Children, I'm sure you know that we've been in a drought for a long time. We desperately need rain. You've probably also heard about Mr. Hatfield, who has been hired by the city of San Diego to produce rain. If you'd like to say something about this, let's hear one of you at a time.

Robert, I saw your hand first, so you begin."

For fifteen minutes the children expressed what they'd heard: Mr. Hatfield is evil. Mr. Hatfield is good. It's not possible to make rain. It is possible to make rain.

"So far, you've told us what you've heard from other people," Carrie explained. "Now I want you to tell us what you think and why you think the way you do."

The faces before her looked puzzled.

"Let me illustrate. Suppose I believe Mr. Hatfield is evil. What reasons do I have for saying that? Have I seen him doing bad things? Or read reports of his evil actions?"

The children frowned, rolled their eyes and still looked confused. Finally, David raised his hand.

"I believe Mr. Hatfield is a scientist."

Surprised, Carrie looked at him and asked, "Why do you believe that?"

"Because I heard he uses chemicals."

"Where did you hear that, David?"

"I heard some men at the store talking about it."

"Very good answer, David. If you were going to write a newspaper story about it, you'd need to get the names and credentials of the people saying those things, wouldn't you?"

David nodded, as did several others.

Carrie prodded the discussion by asking "Does anybody think Mr. Hatfield is evil?"

Three or four hands shot up, and Carrie called on one of the girls.

"He's fooling people. Nobody can make it rain. Only God can."

The discussion continued while Carrie tried to emphasize the importance of verifying the statements they made. It was an interesting exercise, one that Carrie hoped would guide her students into being careful thinkers and engaged citizens of their community.

That evening, Jennie told her family about the discussion they'd had in their classroom that day. "Miss Wyngate said we should have reasons for what we believe and say."

"Your teacher is very right about that," Jennie's father said. "Too many people open their mouths and say things they haven't really thought through."

"What do you think, Daddy. Can people make rain?"

James sat still for a minute. "I don't know, Jennie. I haven't studied into the subject, and I haven't seen it happen. That doesn't mean it's not possible. I guess what I'm saying is that I don't know enough about it, so I'll have to wait and see."

"That's what I think, too, Daddy," Jennie said and ran into the next room to play with her doll.

Chapter Twenty-eight

On January 9, the San Diego Union ran a feature story about the weather. It said nothing about Mr. Hatfield focusing instead on a weather bureau forecaster's report. Storm centers from the Pacific northwest are moving southeasterly across California," the article said.

The next day, Monday, it began raining in the morning, not long after school started. This time, Carrie's students stayed focused on their studies; at least until a sudden downpour pounded so loudly outside that they all raised their heads.

Rain drummed against the hard earth, drilling little holes in the dirt, throwing up splashes of water and mud. It lessened a bit but not enough for the children to go outside for recess. The playground had turned to mud. It taxed the creative abilities of Carrie, and all the teachers, to come up with activities and games the children could play indoors.

The rain continued all day. Most of the children had not worn boots or raincoats. They would be drenched by the time they reached their homes. Carrie wrapped several layers of paper around the cast on David's arm, then buttoned his coat over it all, hoping it would be enough to keep his arm dry until he reached home.

"I'm walking part of the way with him," Charlie said.

"Good. Do your best to keep that cast dry," Carrie said to both boys.

Carrie hadn't worn any rain gear that day, either. She buttoned her coat around herself, found a scarf in her pocket and tied it over her head. Trying to avoid the largest puddles, she tiptoed homeward, arriving with wet feet, wet hair and mud splattered on her skirt.

Bertie had a pot of soup simmering on the stove and a fire burning in the fireplace. Carrie changed out of her wet garments into dry ones and pulled a chair close to the fire. She looked out the window at the steadily falling rain. Bertie joined her.

"We're getting the rain we prayed for."

"Or, according to some people, the rain Mr. Hatfield is making." Carrie gave Bertie a sly grin and watched the older woman for a reaction. Bertie raised her chin and said, "I prefer to give God the credit."

It rained all night. Carrie dug a raincoat and umbrella out of her trunk. She had no boots, so she wore a pair of old shoes and carried another pair to change into when she got to school. Only half her students showed up, many parents choosing to keep their children home. She didn't blame them.

The storm abated late in the day. The following two days, the skies cleared somewhat, prompting several housewives to do a washing and hang it on the backyard lines to dry. Friday morning, just before dawn, a cloudburst battered the roofs of Chula Vistans. Carrie crawled out of bed, walked to the window and looked out. It was like standing behind a waterfall. Rain fell in torrents, making it impossible to see beyond the edge of the yard.

Carrie stayed home that day as did nearly everyone else in Chula Vista. For four days, the deluge continued with no letup. Then, it slackened to steady rain. Streams and rivers overflowed their banks, low places in fields became lakes and streets became so muddy they were nearly impassable.

People tried to maintain normalcy in their lives. Carrie sloshed through the rain and mud every day to school, but classrooms were largely empty of students. News filtered in that the entire county of San Diego had been affected by the unusual amount of rain. The San Diego River overran its banks and flooded Mission Valley. In the south county, officials saw the water levels behind the Sweetwater and Otay dams rise to dangerous levels.

No one knew if the Hatfield brothers were still doing experiments on their tower near the Morena Reservoir, though a dam worker vowed the two men were still up there. A half dozen men hiked up the mountain with the intent of lynching Charles and Joel. They found no one at the testing site. The rainmakers had snuck down the mountain in the brush even as their attackers climbed up the trail.

On January 27, the rain became extremely heavy again. By this time, all schools had been closed for several days. Mr. Rudolph Wueste, in charge of the Otay dam, watched the water level rise and opened the outlet gate to relieve the pressure. This action did nothing to check the rise in the water level. He guessed that the dam would be overtopped before evening; and he telegraphed authorities in both San Diego and Chula Vista.

Men were dispatched to the Otay valley to warn inhabitants to evacuate. The telephone exchange in National City also sent out word. Nate was at City Hall when the alarm was sounded. He volunteered to go.

"I'll drive my truck as far as I can. It could be useful in getting people and their belongings out of there."

He jumped in his truck and slowly maneuvered through the mud on Third Avenue. The tires slipped, and the truck lurched from side to side. He jockeyed the steering wheel back and forth and coaxed the vehicle to keep going. The window wipers were useless in keeping the windshield clear. Nate squinted into the sheets of rain, trying to see any semblance of a road before him. He slithered south toward the Otay river, which had spread itself far beyond its bounds. Seeing a house ahead, he jumped out of his car, banged on the door and yelled for the occupants to leave immediately. A Japanese man came to the door, a confused look in his eyes. A boy squeezed in beside him and translated to his father. The man called out to his wife and other children, who grabbed some blankets and ran out the door, past Nate's truck and toward a nearby hill.

Nate was already in his truck and on his way to the next house. "Get out! The dam is breaking! Get into my truck!" A father, mother and five children climbed into his truck and draped blankets over their heads to keep off the rain.

The road beyond had become totally impassable. Nate turned his vehicle around and headed back the way he came, picking up the Japanese family.

At 4:45 p.m. on Thursday, January 27, water overflowed the Otay dam. Mr. F. E. Baird, one of a group of five men sent to warn valley residents, made it six miles down the valley from the dam. He saw the steel diaphragm of the dam tear from the top down, splitting open like two gates opening outward. A wall of water tore down the valley, roaring, crashing, ripping the life out of the land. Mr. Baird swam for his life. His four companions did not survive.

From above the dam, Mr. Wueste watched the steel core part in the middle, the flood slipping out into the gorge almost soundlessly. As a helpless onlooker, he watched the entire dam structure wear down as the water cut an immense V-shaped gap. By 9 p.m. the dam was totally gone, the sides of the gorge scoured clean up to seventy feet high.

Within 48 minutes, the torrent covered ten miles carrying houses, barns, cattle, trees, crops and people to destruction. By the time the monstrous wall of water reached the communities closest to the bay, the noise was deafening. One survivor said he "heard a great roar, a crash, a boom and a mighty swish. The wall of water seemed to be a hundred feet high. Before I knew it, the water was upon me."

Nate heard the noise, too. It was dark. He could see very little, but he heard the sounds of buildings cracking as they fell before the deluge. The flood roared in his ears like a lion about to spring on its prey.

Carrie stood in the living room listening to Mr. Owens describe what he had heard in town. "The Otay dam collapsed about 5 p.m. today. The valley is destroyed. Messengers were sent out earlier in the day to warn people. Hopefully, everyone got out."

Mr. Owens paused and looked straight at Carrie. "Nate was one of the messengers."

Carrie gasped and her hand flew to her mouth. "Are you sure?"

"The mayor said Nate came into City Hall this morning, heard the news and volunteered to help evacuate people."

Carrie felt her knees go weak. She sat down in a chair. Her chest rose and fell erratically. Her heart pounded so hard, she felt it in her temples. Bertie came to her and touched her shoulder. "I'm sure he's alright. He went out there early in the day and is probably back home by now."

Bertie's words did not comfort her.

James Landon told his wife about his fears for Nate's safety. He didn't know if he should tell his parents, but finally decided he should. "Better they know now than later," he said to Helen as he walked back out into the storm toward his parents' house.

"What's wrong?" his mother asked as soon as he stepped into their home. James recounted the news about the collapse of the Otay dam. Trying to keep his voice steady, he told of Nate's trip to the valley earlier in the day to warn and help evacuate people. Mr. Landon stood silently for a minute, while his wife started dabbing her eyes with a handkerchief. When

Mr. Landon found his voice, he said, "It sounds like something he'd do." He blinked his eyes. "Of course, we don't know anything right now about where he is. Chances are he's on his way home, even as we speak."

Mrs. Landon nodded. "I think we should pray for his safety." She bowed her head, reached for her husband's hand and said, "God, you know where our son is. He went out to help others. Protect him."

Mr. Landon and James both added short prayers for Nate's safety. James said he needed to get back to his own family and keep them calm in this storm. "I'll let you know if I hear anything," he promised as he opened the door and stepped out into the storm.

The Landons sank into their chairs before the fireplace, where they stayed for most the night. Too concerned to sleep, they dozed in between stoking the fire with wood.

Chapter Twenty-nine

The next day, Friday, citizens of Chula Vista rallied to help storm victims. A shelter was set up in the packing plant on Third Avenue. Donations began flooding in: blankets, towels, toothbrushes, soap, food. As soon as Carrie heard of it, she signed up as a volunteer. She needed something to do to beat back her anxiety about Nate.

A reporter came by in the middle of the day and took pictures of the volunteers helping flood survivors. Throughout the day, more details about the disaster unfolded. The Sweetwater dam did not break, but overflowed, devastating the Sweetwater and Bonita valleys. The flood took out homes and buildings, destroyed railroad tracks, bridges and roads, cutting off all connections between Chula Vista and National City or San Diego to the north. The flood in the Otay valley cut off Chula Vista on the south side. The city was isolated. With telegraph lines down and roads closed, communication came to a stand-still.

Most of Little Landers was gone, and Carrie remembered the idyllic little community she and the Owenses had driven through last October.

Victims of the flood arrived at the shelter with harrowing stories. Mr. Henry Clay George had been one of two volunteers to warn people in Otay valley. His youngest child was less than a year old, yet Mr. George left home and rode bareback on his horse for many miles in the rain. One of the last homes he and his friend visited was the Daneri home, where they were invited to stay for dinner.

Mr. George declined, saying he needed to get home to his own family. His decision saved his life. The host, Manuel Daneri, descended into a big, cement wine cellar not far from the house to get drinks. His wife stepped out of the house to call him for dinner, but as he climbed the steps out of the wine cellar, he and she both saw a wall of water bearing down on them. Husband and wife ran up the hill, shouting to the others inside the house to come out. They didn't hear the warning, and the house and at least eight people, including Mr. George's friend who had come to warn them, all died.

Carrie shuddered when she heard the story. She had to grit her teeth from crying out as her mind conjured up Nate washed away in the flood, his body swept into the bay. That was another piece of information that came to the shelter: bodies found in the bay. Other bodies unaccounted for, particularly a group of eight or nine Japanese farmers.

In the makeshift kitchen of the shelter, Carrie stirred a big pot of soup, keeping her head down to hide the tears that continually rose to her eyes. She finally got herself under control and began dipping the soup into bowls. After lunch, she was sweeping the floor when someone tapped her on the shoulder.

Carrie spun around. "Mary, you startled me. I didn't see you come in."

The usually convivial Mary looked troubled, her forehead crinkled with worry lines.

"Have you heard? Charlie Jenkins is missing."

"Charlie? He lives in town. How could he be caught in the flood?"

"Some children saw him running last evening in the rain. They said that he told them he was going to see if his friend David was alright."

Thoughts tumbled in Carrie's mind. Charlie? David? Carrie felt faint. Mary grabbed her arm to steady her.

"You need to sit down. Let's go over there." Mary pointed to some chairs against the wall. The two women walked to them, Mary guiding Carrie by the elbow. As soon as they sat down, Mary disclosed more information.

"I heard this in town, stopped by the Jenkins' home to verify it and felt you needed to hear it from someone you know, rather than a stranger."

Carrie couldn't speak and Mary continued.

"You know the Imamuras live out toward Bonita."

Carrie nodded. "I walked out there once."

"Charlie got it in his head that they might be in danger from the flood, so he ran off in that direction."

"The Imamuras live on the side of a hill. Surely the water didn't come up that far."

"You're correct. The Imamuras are safe, though not far below their place, the whole valley is a huge, muddy lake."

"You're sure about this?"

"Absolutely. I talked with Mr. Jenkins half an hour ago. He was out all night looking for Charlie and again this morning. He found the Imamuras, but they had not seen Charlie."

Carrie dropped her head, put her hands over her face and cried. Mary reached out a hand and patted her on the shoulder. "I know this is bad news."

"It's...it's awful." Carrie's shoulders shook. Then she lifted her head and looked at Mary. "How about Mrs. Jenkins... and... and...Mr. Jenkins?"

"Very upset, as you can imagine, but Mr. Jenkins says he's not giving up. He's going to comb every corner of the community until he finds his son."

"Does he have anyone to help him?"

"Friends and neighbors."

"I'd like to help," Carrie found herself saying.

"I think the best help you and I could give is to stay with Mrs. Jenkins awhile."

"Let me see if I can leave my post here at the shelter." Carrie stood and looked around. "Bertie is here somewhere. I'll ask if she can fill in for me."

Minutes later, Carrie and Mary were slogging through the muddy streets toward the Jenkins' home. They knocked on the door and a little boy, who looked so much like Charlie that it took Carrie's breath away, opened the door. His mother came up behind the boy. "May I help you?"

"Hello, Mrs. Jenkins. I'm Charlie's teacher, Miss Wyngate, and this is my friend, Mary, who teaches first grade. We came by to see if there is any way we can help you and your family."

Tears came to Mrs. Jenkins eyes and she motioned them in. "Come in. Come in. I don't know how you can help, but it's kind of you to come."

They stood in the hallway, not knowing what to say to each other. "Mrs. Jenkins," Carrie began, "your son, Charlie, is a strong boy. I believe he's out there somewhere and he'll be home...soon."

Mrs. Jenkins dabbed at her eyes. "That's nice of you to say...but...but... he's been gone all night and...half the day."

In her mind, Carrie knew that the odds of a boy of Charlie's age surviving a night in the rain might not be good, yet she willed herself to believe that he could. Somehow. But how?

"I've been so upset," Mrs. Jenkins continued between quiet sobs, "that I've neglected the rest of the family."

Mary stepped forward. "That's how we can help you. Let us look after the younger children for awhile."

Carrie and Mary spent the next two hours playing with the Jenkins' five-year-old son and three-year-old daughter, while Mrs. Jenkins retired to her room to take a nap, which her overwrought emotions denied her. By mid-afternoon, Carrie's mind was running over with worry. The winter sun would set in two hours. It would be dark. Charlie must be found before nightfall.

Chapter Thirty

The door banged open and a voice yelled "Mommy! Mommy! I'm home!"

Carrie and Mary looked up and saw Mr. Jenkins walk in the front door carrying Charlie in his arms. The boy had his arm wrapped around his father's neck.

All of them leaped up and ran toward father and son. Mrs. Jenkins bolted down the stairs, straight to her husband and son, and scooped the boy into her arms, kissing him all over his face. Tears ran down her cheeks.

Mr. Jenkins stood quietly, and Carrie noticed tears in his eyes, too. After the first round of hugs, kisses, laughter and tears, Mr. Jenkins said, "Son, do you want to tell your mother what happened?"

Charlie slid out of his mother's arms and stood straight and tall. "I heard the flood was near my friend David's house. He has a broken arm and I thought he might need help. So I started walking to his house."

Mrs. Jenkins gasped, and her husband put his finger to his lips and said, "Let the boy continue."

"It was raining really hard and it got dark. I couldn't see and I got lost." Charlie fidgeted with his fingers. "I saw a house with a candle on a table by the window, so I went to the door and knocked."

"Oh, my dear boy," Mrs. Jenkins said as she dabbed her eyes again.

"An old lady came to the door. I said I was lost and she said come in. So I did. She took off my wet clothes and wrapped a blanket around me and made me sit next to the stove. She fed me some soup, too, and a biscuit."

"God bless her," Mrs. Jenkins said.

"I guess I went to sleep, 'cause next thing it was morning."

"The lady lives alone," Mr. Jenkins interjected. "She has no transportation or way of communicating, so she had no option except to keep our son overnight and no way of telling anyone. Her grandson stops by once a day. He arrived in the early afternoon, heard the story and brought Charlie to City Hall hoping someone would know where he belonged. The mayor sent scouts out looking for me. And here we are." The tears in Mr. Jenkins' eyes had spilled down his face. He reached out to Charlie and drew him close again.

Carrie brushed tears out of her eyes, too, and said ,"I'm so glad you're home, Charlie." She patted the boy on his head and he looked up at her. "You know what the best thing is, teacher?"

"What?"

"David is safe. The flood didn't get him."

"I know, Charlie. Isn't that wonderful?"

After a few more minutes of talk, Carrie and Mary excused themselves. Mr. Jenkins walked them to the door; and as Carrie walked past him, he whispered. "Don't worry about the school board. I'm canceling my complaint and working on being a better father."

As Mary and Carrie walked away from the Jenkins' home, Mary said, "Isn't it wonderful that Charlie's been found?"

Carrie agreed by nodding her head. Her voice refused to work.

As they walked back to the shelter, Carrie's heart thrilled with what she'd witnessed at the Jenkins' home. At the same time, she felt sheer terror at what she might hear about Nate.

A group of women were setting out food for supper at the refugee center; and she and Mary joined them. A fire burned in a wood stove in one corner of the big room, and people huddled around it. Carrie noticed there were not as many people as there had been earlier in the day. One of the ladies said that many of the families had gone to stay with other family members or friends.

As they set food on the table, people talked of the day's events. "The military has sent troops down to Otay valley to prevent looting....How awful that there are people who would steal from people who are suffering.... I heard the military has orders to shoot looters on sight....

Did you hear the airplane go over? They sent a photographer up in the air to take pictures of the disaster."

In the middle of the conversations that swirled about them, Mary said she needed to go home. Carrie walked her to the door and thanked her for her friendship and support. Mary walked out into the darkness. Street lamps in town didn't function. Electricity, in the homes that had it, was out. It was a bleak evening. Carrie returned to the hall to help with the after-supper cleanup. Then, she would go home.

She was wiping down the table when the door opened and a family of five, weary-looking people stumbled in, followed by a tall man in muddy clothing and a water-soaked hat that drooped over his forehead. Carrie squinted to see better, then dropped the cleaning cloth on the table, sprinted across the room, yelling "Nate! Nate!" She flung herself at him. He awkwardly caught her and looked down at her upturned face.

"I thought you were—" Sobs cut off what she wanted to say. She tried again. "I thought you were—"

"Dead?" He finished her sentence.

"That I'd never see you again."

"Do you want to see me again?"

"I want to see you every day of my life."

"This is nice to hear," he said. "Does this mean you care about me?"

Carrie winced. He was making it hard, but she wouldn't back away. Not this time. "Yes. And I'm sure about that."

He smiled, drew her closer to himself and hugged her so tight she thought her ribs would crack. People in the room applauded. Nate and Carrie looked up but continued to stand wrapped in each other's arms for several minutes.

"This is the best place in the world to be," Nate whispered in her ear, "but do you suppose we can get some food for that family I brought in? And some blankets?"

Carrie stood back. "Yes, of course! And you need something to eat, too."

Within minutes, Nate had directed the family to the table, and Carrie was serving them food. Then, she rummaged in the donation boxes in the back of the room and came up with bedding for all of them. As she worked, she kept looking toward Nate. Even in his rain-sopped clothing, he looked good. She felt such happiness inside that she couldn't stop smiling.

Once the family had been taken care of, she turned to Nate. "Do you need a place to stay or are you going home?"

"I'm going home as soon as I can get away from this woman who keeps hanging onto me." He grinned.

"Would you mind giving me a ride to the Owenses' house?"

"Not at all, but you'll have to ride on my shoulders."

Carrie saw the twinkle in his eyes and asked, "What do you mean?"

"I don't have a car. It's stuck in the mud up to the axles several miles south of here."

"How did you and those people get here?"

"Walked."

"How do you plan to get home?"

"Walk."

"You must be exhausted. You can't walk home. It's still quite a ways."

"I know, but do you have any other suggestions?"

"Let's walk together to the Owenses' house. We'll figure it out from there."

Minutes later, Nate and Carrie were walking, hand in hand, down F Street. When they opened the Owenses' front door, Bertie and Archie leaped from their chairs and hurried toward them.

"Oh, Nate, It's so good to see you," Bertie said as she hugged him.

Mr. Owens placed his hand on Nate's shoulder. "We've been mighty worried about you."

Bertie loosened her embrace and said, "Let me get some coffee." She turned toward the kitchen. Carrie followed.

Bertie filled the coffee pot with water and set it on the stove. "You look happy, Carrie."

"Oh, Bertie, I am happy. I was so scared that Nate had drowned..."

"But he didn't, and you realized through all this that you care about him... a lot."

"How did you know?"

Bertie laughed. "As the saying goes, 'I've been around the teacup long enough to find the handle.'"

Carrie giggled.

"And I've learned one other thing." Bertie looked serious. "When you find the handle, hang onto it."

The women finished making coffee, spread cookies on a platter and carried the refreshments to the living room. As they sat around the fire drinking coffee and eating cookies, Mr. Owens looked at Nate and asked, "Please share with us what happened the last two days."

Nate took a deep breath and reviewed how he warned the Japanese family, how he put the other family in his truck and drove up the hill. "There was a house up there, with a light in it. So I stopped and asked the folk if we could take refuge in their home. I was pretty sure it was high enough so the water would not reach us. Everyone squeezed into that little living room. I was the last one to go in. Standing on the front porch, I heard the flood roaring down the valley. That's when I wondered if we were out of harm's way."

"It was a really loud noise?" Mr. Owens asked.

"Deafening. I never heard anything like it and hope I never will again."

Carrie had her eyes pinned on Nate's face and saw a flicker of the terrifying experience reflected in his eyes. No one said anything for a few seconds, then Nate continued his story.

"Obviously, we were safe or I wouldn't be here telling you about it. When we got up in the morning and saw how close the flood had come, it scared me all over again. All I wanted to do was get out of there."

"I bet." Mr. Owens reached for a cookie. "How close was it?"

"Three hundred yards or so."

"Oh, my!" Bertie exclaimed.

Nate took a sip of coffee. "I loaded both the Japanese family and the other family into my truck and started driving, but the mud was thick and slippery. Next thing I knew, the truck slid in a ditch. We worked for hours trying to get it out, pushing, shoving, laying boards under the tires.

Nothing worked. So we left it and started walking to Chula Vista."

Bertie shook her head. "I can't believe you all walked that far, especially those children and their mothers."

"We had to take it pretty slow; but anyway, here I am, mud and all." Nate brushed at the dirt on his pants. "Looking pretty despicable. Thanks for taking me in and listening to my adventure. I need to head home. I know the folks are worried about me."

Carrie rose from her chair and stepped toward Nate. "I'm sorry I detained you. How thoughtless of me!"

"I chose to stay," Nate said as he stood and moved toward the door.

Mr. Owens set his coffee cup down. "You're not walking home, Nate Landon. Not after all you've been through. I'll drive you."

"I don't want to inconvenience you."

"It's what friends and neighbors are for," Mr. Owens said, "and it looks to me like we're all going to have to pull together quite a bit to dig our way out of this disaster."

A few minutes later, Carrie and Bertie walked the men to the door and urged them to drive carefully. Nate took Carrie's hand and whispered in her ear. "I'll be over tomorrow. I think we have a lot to talk about."

Chapter Thirty-one

Nate was so tired when he crawled in bed that night that he immediately fell asleep. When he awoke the next morning, his mind raced with happy thoughts about Carrie, then troubled ones because he felt so unprepared financially. The recent flood would likely make it even more difficult to save money. He needed to asses the lemon orchard. Had the rain affected it positively or negatively? He reflected on how the flood had already changed his life. It had brought him and Carrie together. That made him smile, then frown as he considered how to pursue his relationship with her.

As he usually did in difficult situations, he chose work to clear his head. As soon as he ate breakfast, he walked to his brother's house, where he asked if James could drive him south to where his truck was stuck in the mud. James agreed and they set out.

"Could you stop at the Owenses' house for just a minute?" he asked as they drove toward the center of town.

"Sure." James looked at Nate, but Nate kept his eyes straight ahead.

"I need to speak with Carrie a minute."

"So you two are on speaking terms again." James had turned onto F Street. He slowed to a stop in front of the Owenses' house. Nate jumped out of the car and bounded up the front steps two at a time.

When Carrie appeared, he wanted to grab her in his arms and whisk her away with him. Instead, he apologized for not having time to talk with her right now because he needed to rescue his truck. "Ride along with me," he heard himself ask.

"You want me to help push your truck out of the mud?" she teased.

"Definitely. Isn't that what you put on the calendar to do today?"

Carrie laughed. "If you'll stop by the rescue center first so I can see if they need me or not, then there's a possibility that I can join you in playing in the mud."

A few minutes later, Carrie hopped into the car and James swung by the rescue center. There were fewer clients today. They didn't need her, so she rode with James and Nate. They stopped at a farm house not far from Nate's truck and hired a farmer with a tractor to help.

The tractor chugged slowly behind them until they reached the ditch containing the stranded truck. Carrie's eyes swept the landscape in all directions, taking in the devastation. Straight ahead, the valley looked like a battlefield, the brown river waters still carrying tree limbs, boards and other debris. Where the water had already receded along the banks, the skeletal remains of houses and sheds stood at rakish angles.

"This is terrible," Carrie said. "Worse than I imagined."

"I agree with you," James said as he stopped the car.

The farmer with the tractor made a U-turn in the road and backed towards Nate's truck. James and Nate immediately joined the farmer in hitching up a cable from the tractor to the truck. Carrie stayed in the car and watched. The farmer hopped back onto the tractor, shifted gears and put his foot on the gas. The engine clattered and strained. Slowly, it began to move forward. The cable pulled taut. The truck in the ditch seemed to quiver, then move slowly, inch by inch as the farmer coaxed more power out of the tractor. Finally, the truck stood on the road, freed from the ditch, caked in mud up to the door handles.

The three men unhitched the car, rolled up the cable and the man on the tractor headed homeward. James drove away, too, leaving Nate and Carrie to climb carefully into the muddy truck. Nate wanted to drive to the house where he and his refugees had spent the night. "I want to thank them again."

Within minutes, Carrie and Nate stood on the front porch. They were greeted with smiles and invited in. For several minutes, the family talked of the flood and the damage all around them. "Our fields are gone, but we are fortunate to be alive and have a roof over our heads," they said. "Look at that valley down there. Many people lost everything. Houses. Livestock. Everything. Some lost their lives."

Nobody said anything for a few minutes, then the man of the house said. "There is a lot of wreckage up here on the high ground, too. There are houses that are damaged and need immediate repair."

Nate nodded as his mind swirled with an idea, and he found himself saying, "I'm a pretty good repairman. Maybe I could help."

Within minutes, his host supplied him with a list of names and directions. He and Carrie returned to the truck and drove to each one of the homes on the list, assessing damage, offering assistance. Nate compiled a shopping list of supplies, and when they drove back to town, he made a beeline for the hardware store. It wasn't until he stood at the cash register that he wondered how he would pay for these supplies. He felt embarrassed when Mr. Shafer announced the total, especially in Carrie's hearing.

"Uh, Mr. Shafer, I...I...don't—"

Mr. Shafer cut him off. "It's alright, Nate. We'll put it on a special account to be settled up later."

"Oh. Thank you."

Nate carried the supplies to his truck, Carrie following him. As they drove away, she said, "It's wonderful what you're doing, Nate. I was thinking maybe we could start a drive to raise funds."

Her words made a lump rise in his throat. Carrie understood him. If he hadn't been driving, he would have kissed her right then and there. Even thinking about kissing Carrie made his heart race.

"Thank you, Carrie."

They drove in silence for a few minutes, then Nate said, "Maybe I should take you home now, because you'll probably get bored following me around making repairs on people's houses."

"I'd never get bored with you; but I probably wouldn't be very useful to you."

"You don't have to be useful to be useful to me," he said as he turned the steering wheel sharply to miss a sunken spot in the road.

Nate drove to the Owenses' house and escorted Carrie to the front door. He hated leaving her and promised to return in the evening. "I can't do any work after dark, anyway," he said. "Besides, we still have a lot to talk about."

She tipped her head and looked into his eyes as he touched her cheek with his finger and said, "I'll be back."

As soon as he drove away, he began thinking about what he thought they needed to talk about. He wanted answers to her fearful allusions to Chicago. What had happened to her before she came here? Suddenly, the thought came to him that she might want to know more about him, too. He had nothing to hide, except his shaky financial situation. Nate was quite sure he did not want to talk about that with Carrie.

A more troubling and immediate problem rose in his mind. Where could he and Carrie talk together privately? Not in the Owenses' front room. Not at his parent's home. They couldn't sit on a park bench somewhere. The whole town was as soggy as a wet dog, and the winter evening would be damp and cold.

He wrinkled his forehead as he realized his desires clashed with his realities.

Carrie fluffed the sofa cushions and added another log to the fire. Nate would be here any moment. The Owenses had gone to visit friends. She and Nate would be alone to talk.

As soon as he knocked on the door, her heart flipped. She invited him in and directed him to a spot on the sofa, sitting down beside him. He chatted about the repairs he planned to make to the homes ravaged by the flood. The excitement in his voice made her proud that he was a man who was generous, kind and talented.

He reached for her hand and squeezed it. "Sorry, I've been babbling about myself. It's your turn. What have you been doing today?"

She laughed. "I started the day traveling with a man who's obsessed with helping his community and has the brains and abilities to make things happen."

He grinned back at her, then grew serious. "Really, Carrie. I want to know more about you. I know you came from Chicago and that you lost your parents at a young age and your grandmother raised you, but I sense there is something more to that story."

Carrie dropped her eyes and stayed silent. Finally, she began talking in almost a whisper.

"My mom died giving birth to me. My father moved me and himself in with his mother. She took care of me during the day. He was there for me every evening and on weekends." Carrie stopped and took a deep breath before she continued.

"I adored my father. He played with me. Took me to the park on Sunday afternoons. We walked to the corner drug store every Saturday afternoon and bought ice-cream cones. He always introduced me to all his friends and acquaintances. 'This is my beautiful daughter, Carrie.' He was so proud of me."

Again, Carrie paused. She didn't know if she could go on. The next part of the story always made her cry.

"It was winter. I had a new red snowsuit. He promised we'd make a snowman in the park as soon as he came home from work." Carrie sniffed and blinked her eyes.

"He was struck and killed by a car on his way home."

Nate put his arms around Carrie and held her close, stroking her shoulder. She squeezed her eyes shut to keep from crying. Gradually, she got herself under control, opened her eyes and lifted her head.

"Looking back on it, I don't know how my grandmother handled the loss of her son and still had so much love to give to me. She did everything to assure that I had a good life, and she kept the memory of my father and my mother alive for me."

Carrie raised her hand to the locket around her neck. "Grandma bought me this locket and put pictures of my mother and father inside it." She lifted the necklace from her neck, unlatched the locket and opened it for Nate to see.

"My father and grandmother always said I look a lot like my mother."

Nate looked intently at the picture. "You do. You've got her hair and eyes."

Carrie fingered the edges of the locket, then closed it and set it in her lap.

"Grandma took me to museums and concerts. Every week we went to the library and I checked out books. She always asked me questions about what I read. She was a natural-born teacher. Most of all, she loved me. I miss her so much. She died last year just before Mother's Day."

"You've had a lot of losses, Carrie." Nate hugged her tighter. "Is that why you left Chicago? To get away from the sad memories?"

"It was more than that." Carrie twisted her skirt in her fingers. "but I can't talk about it right now. Maybe later, Nate."

They both heard footsteps on the porch. The Owenses were home. Nate and Carrie scooted apart from each other and lifted smiling faces to the Owenses as they walked in.

Nate didn't stay much longer. It wasn't until after he left that Carrie realized she hadn't learned anything about him. She tried to tell herself that it didn't matter because she loved what she did know.

Chapter Thirty-two

Even though storm damage made life difficult in Chula Vista for everyone, school resumed on February 3, a week after the flood. Carrie felt relieved with normalcy restored by regular classes. David and Charlie still sat next to each other, the latter taking care of the written assignments for the other. Charlie became more calm and secure, more able to control his fidgety behavior. He seemed to concentrate better. Carrie attributed the change to the fact that Charlie's father had made a change in his treatment of his son. The close call of almost losing the boy had made Mr. Jenkins a kinder man.

Carrie felt more secure, too, in her relationship with Nate. Yet she realized she needed to know more about the man. It was lack of knowledge that had caused her trouble in Chicago. She didn't want to repeat that mistake.

She decided to ask Mr. Owens his opinion of Nate but couldn't find a time when she could speak to him alone. The opportunity finally came one evening when Bertie left the house to attend a Women's Club meeting. Carrie spent the early part of the evening in her room going over school plans for the next day. When she finished, she wandered downstairs, poured herself a glass of water, returned to the living room and sat across from Mr. Owens, who was reading a book. He looked up long enough to smile and nod her direction.

"Excuse me, Mr. Owens, but I was wondering if I could get your opinion about something."

"Sure. What's going on in that head of yours?" He closed his book and set it in his lap.

Carrie wrapped and unwrapped her fingers around the glass of water. "I was wondering what you might know about the Landon family."

"Fine family. They moved here about twenty years ago. Bought five acres where they built their home and planted a lemon grove. Both the boys attended grade school here, then high school in San Diego. The older boy, James, got a job as manager at a packing plant. He married, bought some land, built a house where they are today."

Carrie ran her finger around the bottom of her glass.

Mr. Owens looked her direction and continued. "The elder Mr. Landon began having health problems—heart, I think; so Nate agreed to take over management of his lemon orchard. In exchange, he would keep all the proceeds, save a nest egg and buy his own piece of land."

Carrie listened intently.

"The big freeze came along and killed off many of the lemon trees. Then, we had a four-year drought. Crops have not been good. Now, we've had this disastrous flood. Nobody knows the damage it has caused. I think Nate's dreams have been put on hold."

"And the father? Is his health any better?

"I think he's doing fairly well. He just can't do the heavy work he used to do. But that Nate is a hard worker, and I hear he's really good with his hands."

"His niece showed me some wooden toys he made for her and her brothers. It was very nice work."

Mr. Owens picked up his book again and opened it.

"Thanks for the information, Mr. Owens. Sounds like they are a normal family with the usual challenges." She took a sip of water and sat still, thinking over what Mr. Owens had said. She was pretty sure he knew why she asked. Mr. Owens disclosed enough, yet not too much, to help her understand that, no matter how much Nate cared for her, he might be unable to move forward into a future with her.

This revelation made her depressed, yet she knew she would not abandon Nate just because his circumstances were not as ideal as he might wish. Everyone had their own set of problems. Nothing in life was perfect. Still, how long would she have to wait to begin a life with Nate?

As soon as she thought about life with Nate, Carrie backed away from the idea, feeling unsure about making that kind of commitment. Then she reproved herself for her hesitation as she remembered the hours of horror she'd experienced when it seemed that Nate had been swept away from her in the flood. Her emotions seemed like a team of mismatched horses unwilling to go in the same direction.

Every evening, Nate's truck pointed in the direction of the Owenses' home where he spent at least an hour visiting with Carrie before he headed toward his home. The Owenses gave them some privacy by keeping themselves in the kitchen on the pretext of drinking coffee and reading the paper at the table.

One evening, while they had a few moments alone, Carrie asked Nate about the New Year's Eve party. "Did you come with Mary?" she asked.

"No. We just happened to arrive at the same time. She and Miguel came together."

"Mary and Miguel?"

"You didn't know? They've been seeing each other quite a bit lately."

"She and you...."

"Never anything there as far as I was concerned. When you came to Chula Vista, that blocked all other women out of my mind." Nate reached for Carrie's hand.

"H-m-m-m-m." Carrie wrinkled her forehead. "Mary and Miguel. Never would have guessed it."

Mr. Owens walked into the living room to stir the fire, interrupting their conversation about Mary. Nate switched topics by talking about the building projects he was involved in.

"There's a house down near the salt works where the water came up on the back porch, so they decided to replace it. I drew up a plan. Which they really liked."

"Did you make it special in some way?"

"I added a rack near the door. A place to set their work shoes before going inside."

"Smart way to keep the floors clean."

Nate smiled. "Just finished building the porch today. You ought to see it. It looks pretty nice."

"I imagine it does. Have you ever thought about building a whole house?"

Nate frowned. "Lots of times, but it's not in the cards right now . . . maybe someday." He dropped his eyes for a second, then raised them to

Carrie. "I helped my dad build the house we live in; also helped with my brother's place. So I know I could do it."

"I'm sure you could."

Nate reveled in Carrie's appreciation of his abilities. It gave him more confidence in himself, and with the current needs in Chula Vista for repairmen and carpenters, he knew he would continue to develop more skill. There would be plenty of work for a long time, repairing storm damage to people's homes. Few could pay him much; some, nothing at all. So, why did he do it? Because the orchards were too sodden to work, and he found joy in fixing things. Maybe it could lead to something more in the future; meanwhile, the gratitude of the people he helped was very satisfying. Folk referred him to their friends and neighbors, keeping him popping in and out of Shafer's hardware and Mike's Lumber Yard so often that both proprietors joked about him being like a revolving door.

One morning in the middle of February when Nate stopped by the hardware store for a supply of nails, Mr. Shafer said, "You've been mighty busy helping folks fix things up, and I hear you do good work."

"Thank you. I enjoy it."

"Looks like there's going to be plenty of repair and construction work going on around here for a long time. I've had so many people coming in here for supplies and advice that I'm about worn out. Mike says the same thing about his lumber yard."

Mr. Shafer ran his hand across his chin. "Mike and I got to talking about how busy we are and we came up with an idea. How would you like to work for us part time, Nate? We need somebody with knowledge about how to do things to wait on customers, maybe even hire out to do jobs. Do you think you could split yourself between my hardware store and Mike's Lumber Yard for a few hours a week during our busiest times? It wouldn't be full-time work, but it would allow you to continue the jobs you're already doing for people."

"I'd love it, Mr. Sitckley! How many hours a week are you thinking?"

"Ten to fifteen."

"I should be able to do that."

"You're sure?" Mr. Shafer leaned over the counter. "Don't want to wear you out."

"I can do it. It will be good experience for me."

"Then it's a deal. Why don't you start first of next week?" Mr. Shafer reached out his hand and they shook.

Chapter Thirty-three

That afternoon, Carrie was walking home from school when Nate's truck pulled up beside her. He stopped and got out, saying, "Finished all my jobs early today and thought you might like to take a little ride with me." He opened the door for her and she climbed in with a smile on her face.

"How's my favorite school teacher?"

Carrie smiled even broader. "Happy to see you and happy to be done for the day."

"Did you have a rough day?"

"No. In fact, the children have been attentive and working hard. Things are going smoothly. Did I tell you how much Charlie has changed?"

"No, but I'm glad to hear it."

"He's really calmed down and seems so much more content. It's amazing what a difference it makes when a child feels loved and appreciated by the parents."

"Mr. Jenkins has really turned over a new leaf?"

"As far as I can tell. It really shook him up when he thought he might have lost his son."

"I guess so. He's a lucky man to have a second chance. What about the Japanese boy? How's he doing?"

"David always does well in school. He's out of his cast now." Carrie set the books and papers she had been carrying on the floor of the truck near her feet. "Did you hear that there are several Japanese people who are unaccounted for since the flood?"

"Actually, I saw some Japanese people in boats the day after the flood. They were paddling around in the bay looking for lost family and friends."

"Really, Nate? You saw them, looking for...." Carrie's voice stuck in her throat. Finally, she was able to whisper, "That's so sad." She pulled a handkerchief from her pocket and blotted her eyes. "The flood has reminded me that all people are the same inside. Same feelings. Same desires. Including the Japanese people."

Nate reached for Carrie's hand. "I know. That Japanese family I helped evacuate...they were very nice. Ever since the flood, I see people in a different way."

Carrie suppressed her surprise at Nate's new perspective and gave a light response. "Me, too. If it hadn't been for the flood, I don't know when I might have realized what a treasure you are." She giggled. "I might have let you get away."

Nate looked at her as he turned the truck in the direction of the bay. "I'm glad you didn't."

As they drove toward the yacht club pier, they saw several people milling about waiting for the next boat to come in. Since the bridges, railroad tracks and roads had been destroyed by the flood, the boat pier had become the transportation hub for Chula Vista. Nate parked the truck so they could view the water. It was gray, like the sky, though there were intermittent breaks in the clouds letting weak shafts of sunlight through. A string of brown pelicans soared inches above the water, their necks curved into S shapes.

Carrie leaned forward in her seat. "Even on a cloudy day, it's beautiful here."

Nate turned toward her. "I have some news to share."

Carrie scooted closer to him. "I hope it's good news. We've had enough of the other kind, lately."

"It is. At least I think it is. Maybe you won't think it's so good."

"Why wouldn't I?"

"I've got a new job. At least a part-time job."

"What kind of job?"

"Mr. Shafer at the hardware store and Mike at the lumber company want me to work for both of them. Split my time between them. I start next Monday."

Carrie squealed. "That's wonderful, Nate! It's the perfect job for you."

"You really think so?"

"Absolutely. You're good with your hands. And with people."

The smile on Nate's face was like that of a boy opening a longed-for Christmas present. He squeezed Carrie's hand. "Thanks for believing in me."

"I'm so happy for you," she whispered as she nuzzled against his neck.

They sat silently for a few minutes watching a boat tie up to the pier and people trudging ashore. Suddenly, a car jostled across the bumpy dirt road, coming to an abrupt stop at the ramp to the pier.

Nate leaned forward and peered through the windshield. "That's James. Wonder what he's doing here?"

They both watched as James exited his car and walked rapidly toward the moored boat. The captain, the last to step onto the pier, approached James and handed over a package. James didn't stop to talk but hurriedly returned to his car.

"Excuse me, Carrie, I've got to find out what James is up to."

Nate opened the door, jumped out of the truck and trotted across the sand, waving his arms and yelling "James! James!"

Carrie watched as the brothers met and exchanged a few words before James climbed into his car and sped away. Nate ran back to her and leaped into the truck, starting the engine and putting it in reverse before he said a word.

"Is something wrong?"

"I hope not," Nate said as he turned the steering wheel and pointed the truck away from the pier. He kept his eyes on the road while Carrie kept her eyes on him and waited for him to say something more. Finally, he did. "It's Dad."

"Is he sick?"

"He has a heart condition. Takes medication every day. During the flood, he ran out but got a limited supply from the pharmacy. Then, with all the roads and railroad tracks washed away, the pharmacy ran out, too. He's been without for a few days."

"Oh, no!" Carrie said as she put her hand to her mouth. "That's not good."

Nate briefly shifted his head toward her. "We've been watching him closely. As soon as telegraph service was restored, the pharmacy ordered more medication from San Diego. James was here to pick it up."

"Then everything is going to be alright?" Carrie noticed a tremor in her voice and tried to steady herself and reassure both of them by saying, "I'm sure he'll be fine, now."

"I hope so, but when James stopped by the house an hour ago, Dad was feeling weak and out of breath. He hurried to the pharmacy. Heard the shipment was coming in. Came down here so he could get it to Dad as fast as possible." Nate took a deep breath and expelled it in a shudder.

Carrie patted his arm. "You need to be with your father. "Drop me off at my place and go home."

He slowed the truck, pulled into the Owenses' driveway, parked and walked Carrie to the front door. He faced her, took her hands in his and said, "I hadn't planned for our time today to end like this. I wanted to talk... about—"

"Later, Nate. Keep me informed about your father. Please." As Carrie turned from him, she wondered what he might have wanted to talk about. She muffled the question, walked inside the house and shut the door quietly behind her. Standing still, she listened to Nate's retreating footsteps across the porch and down the steps. When you love someone, she thought, it gathers you into their pain and their joy. In less than an hour, she and Nate had shared the happiness of a new job and the fright of an ailing parent. She felt closer to him because of it.

As Carrie walked across the living room and up the stairs to her room, she felt the carefully constructed axis of her life shifting. A painful self-revelation stopped her halfway up the stairs. She stood still, breathing heavily in and out, realizing that the walls she'd erected to protect herself from pain had shut her off from intimacy. With a shudder, she remembered the time Nate had accused her of being heartless. He was partially right. She had a heart, but she'd locked it away so securely no one could peek inside, not even herself. Until now.

Taking a deep breath, she ascended the rest of the stairs, entered the room and set her books and papers on the desk under the window. It's time to let Nate know the whole story about Chicago. If he really loved her, sharing would not scare him away. It would bring them closer, just as the crisis about his father had done. She wanted to talk with Nate as soon as possible, but with the uncertainty of Mr. Landon's health, she knew she'd have to wait.

"God, heal Mr. Landon," she found herself whispering, then amending, "Forgive me if I asked out of my own selfish desires."

Chapter Thirty-four

When Nate swung into the driveway in his truck, he noticed his brother's and the doctor's cars both parked in front of the house. He drove past them and around to the back of the house, where he parked close to the back porch, simultaneously switching off the engine and opening the door. Running toward the porch, he leaped up the steps, then stopped when he reached the door to remove his hat, smooth his jacket, and take a deep breath. He was scared of what he'd find inside.

Walking across the kitchen, he heard soft voices, followed the sound to his parent's bedroom and quietly opened the door. His father lay on his bed, his face sallow against the pillow. The doctor sat beside him, taking his pulse. Nate's mother stood on the opposite side, her lips a tight line. James stood stiffly at the foot of the bed. They looked toward Nate and motioned him closer. Nate tiptoed forward, feeling like it was his own heart that was ill.

"The pulse is regular again," the doctor announced. "You'll need several days of bed rest, Mr. Landon."

Nate's father moaned, and his wife patted his hand. "Now, William, we're going to do as the doctor says."

"I hate...lying in...bed," he mumbled.

Nate almost smiled. His dad couldn't be too bad if he was able to complain.

The doctor dropped his stethoscope into a leather satchel, stood and said, "Continue the medication dosage as before. I'll check in on you tomorrow."

After the doctor left, the family stood around the bed reviewing Mr. Landon's medical condition. Slowly, the color returned to the man's face and his eyes brightened. Finally, he lifted his hand from the bedding and said in a steady voice, "Enough about me. Let's talk about something else."

They all smiled, and James said, "Good idea, Dad. What shall we talk about?"

"Here's some good news," Nate interjected. "I've got a new job." He described the offer he'd been made at the lumber and hardware stores that morning. His parents congratulated him, while James slapped Nate on the shoulders and said, "Well now, you can start thinking about asking Carrie to—"

Nate jerked away. "I told Carrie about the job. She's happy for me."

"Bet she'd be even happier with a ring." James smirked.

"All in due time," Nate replied.

"Well, don't wait too long. You don't want this one to get away."

Nate shook his head as he stepped past his brother and headed for the door. "I'm kind of hungry. Can I fix something for all of us to eat?"

"Dinner time already?" James asked. "I'd better head for home. Helen will be worried."

Mr. Landon lifted his head from the pillow. "Thanks, Son, for your help today."

James stepped closer and grasped his father's hand.

"Rest well tonight, Dad. I'll stop by in the morning on my way to work to see how you're doing."

James let himself out the front door while Nate walked into the kitchen, feeling like life might be returning to normal. His father communicated. His brother teased. Nate searched for food that could be prepared quickly and found leftover stew which he heated. He sliced some bread, poured glasses of milk, and served his parents in their bedroom while he ate alone in the kitchen. He needed solitary time to process the events of the day. The terror that gripped him when he first heard of his father's medical crisis had abated. Tentacles of uncertainty still crawled in his mind. He pushed them back by remembering that the color in his dad's face was better and he talked normally.

Nate turned his thoughts to the positive by imagining what his new job would be like, which led to daydreaming of a time when he might own his own business. What could be more fun than being paid to make or fix things? It suddenly came to him that he'd rather be in a woodworking shop than an orchard.

Holding his soup spoon in mid-air, he gazed at the kitchen wall and muttered, "So, why am I working the soil?" Immediately, he knew the answer. It had been a practical choice. The land was here, so work it. Then heart trouble slowed his father, and the choice was confirmed. Today, his father's health grabbed his attention as never before. The choice would be solidified. Chiseled in stone. Unchangeable. For a moment, Nate felt trapped, as if a door had slammed shut in his face, then he smiled as he realized that Mike and Mr. Shafer had cracked the door open. He could squeeze himself into a new life. It would take time and a double amount of work, but he could do it.

Nate pushed his chair back, picked up his empty dishes and carried them to the sink. What about Carrie? How much financial security did she need? He knew what he'd always expected of himself: ownership of a house and land. Money in a savings account. As he ran water into the dishpan, he questioned if these were reasonable goals. He thought they were, but achieving them would be a long time coming.

Nate slapped the dishcloth against a plate. I can't wait.

He frowned at the impasse he'd created for himself. Love had pushed him into a corner that he didn't know how to get out of. He rinsed the plate, set it on the rack and decided to ask Carrie to marry him. Together, they'd figure out how to live. The decision was like leaping off a cliff and plummeting earthward. Just when he thought he'd reached the craziest conclusion of his life, the updraft of an insight caught him. It was that word: together. He didn't have to figure everything out by himself. He and Carrie could do this—together.

A few minutes later, Nate walked out of the kitchen, feeling such joy inside that he chuckled slightly as he entered his parents' room.

His mother asked, "What are you chortling about?"

"Just happy, I guess."

"That's good," his father added in a voice stronger than it had been an hour ago. "Happiness is worth more than gold." He cleared his throat and continued. "That's what your mother and I have learned."

Nate's mother reached for her husband's hand and squeezed it. William and Agnes smiled and looked into each other's eyes in such a way that Nate felt like an intruder. He backed out of the room and tiptoed to the kitchen, balancing plates and bowls on his arms.

That's what I want for Carrie and me, he thought.

Chapter Thirty-five

A scream jolted Nate awake. He bolted to a sitting position.

"Nate. Come. Quick." It was his mother's voice. In one motion, he vaulted out of bed, shoved one leg, then the other, into his trousers, stumbled over his feet, balanced himself, grabbed a shirt and tried to button it as he ran down the stairs barefooted.

The hall clock chimed five as he hurtled into his parents' room. His mother had one arm under her husband, trying to elevate his head. Nate leaped toward the bed.

"It's his breathing again," his mother gasped. "Help me lift his head."

Nate leaned into his father, whose face was gray. His eyes were shut, his breathing sparse. Nate slid his arms around his father and pulled him into a sitting position while his mother piled pillows behind him. He and his mother stared at the man who suddenly appeared very small to Nate. Seconds, minutes, an eternity passed before the shallow inhalations took on a more regular beat.

"Come on, William," his mother coaxed as she stroked her husband's hand. His eyes fluttered open, unfocused, roving. "I'm right here," she whispered. Gradually, his eyes settled on her face. "You're going to be alright."

"He's going to be alright," she repeated to Nate.

Nate felt nauseous. He put his hand over his eyes and breathed slowly in and out, trying to calm himself. It didn't work. He turned his face toward the door so his parents couldn't see the tears leaking onto his cheeks. It took forever, it seemed, before he could look at them again.

Nate cleared his throat. "I'm going to James' place. Ask him to come stay with you while I get the doctor."

As sick as he was, Nate's father crinkled his eyebrows together in disagreement.

"Good idea," his mother said.

By 8 a.m., the Landon family had reorganized their lives. The doctor had come and gone, emphasizing again that the patient needed strict bed rest, light food and a quiet atmosphere. Mr. Landon was breathing easily, his pulse steady. Helen and the baby would stay with William and Agnes while James took the older children to school and himself to work. Nate had a job to complete on one of the flood damaged homes. He would return as soon as he could. An unspoken pact had been agreed upon that William and Agnes Landon would not be alone. A family member would always be with them.

Though Nate agreed wholeheartedly with the plan, he worried about his new job starting on Monday, about finding time with Carrie, about the people depending on him to repair their damaged homes. He felt overwhelmed.

He stopped by the school at 8:45, something he had never done, and found Carrie writing assignments on the blackboard. When he spoke her name, she whirled around, her eyes wide and her mouth open. "It's your father. He's—"

'He's alright," Nate said quietly. "At least, for now." Quickly, he told her about the events of the previous evening and early morning.

"I'm sorry, Nate."

"I'm more than sorry. I'm worried."

"I know how you feel," she said. "Is there anything I can do to help?"

"Just wait for me. I don't know how much I'll be able to see you for awhile."

"I'll always be here for you."

Nate wished he could take her in his arms, but of course he couldn't. Not here. School would start in a few minutes. "I'll be in touch as often as I can," he said as he struggled to contain his emotions. He dug his fingers into the palms of his hands and backed away. At the doorway, he managed a slight smile before he disappeared down the hallway.

Carrie stood still. Fixed in place. Unable to move. Overcome with concern and sadness. The school bell rang, jangling her into her responsibilities for the day. She put a smile on her face to greet her students when they arrived.

The day seemed unending. Thoughts of the Landon family kept her from being completely engaged in teaching. When the closing bell rang, Carrie dismissed the children quickly and hurried out of the classroom nearly as fast as they did. Once she turned onto F Street, she slowed, not wanting her body to arrive at the Owenses' home before her mind was prepared to share information about the Landons. Bertie would be eager to talk, not that Carrie disliked that trait in the woman. It's just that she wanted time alone to consider what to do to help Nate. She could think of nothing. Instead, the illness of Nate's father stirred up memories of Chicago, less than a year ago: a warm and sunny day two weeks before Mother's Day.

That afternoon, Carrie had helped her students make Mother's Day cards, then she had walked to her rooming house, delighting in flowers blooming in window-boxes and birds twittering in the trees. She made a salad for supper and had barely finished eating it when there was a knock on the door. She opened to a neighbor of her grandmother's. The look on his face frightened her.

"What's wrong?"

"Your grandmother. She's had a stroke."

Two hours later, Carrie sat beside a hospital bed, holding her grandmother's limp hand and looking at her face, the left side of the mouth drooping, the eyes closed, and apparently the ears, too.

"Unresponsive," the medical people said.

Carrie talked to her anyway. "I love you, Grandma. Please get well."

For hours, she sat, speaking to her grandmother about the good times they'd had and the good times they could still have. "I'll take care of you," she whispered as she leaned over her grandmother and kissed her on the cheek, crying big tears that splattered onto the bed covers. She watched the shallow rise and fall of Grandma's chest. Stroked the pale, wrinkled hands and prayed, "God, please don't let her go. I need her."

Shortly after midnight, the faint breathing stopped for a few seconds, resumed again, then stopped forever.

The nurses let Carrie stay awhile longer, then led her away, offering her medication to "help her cope," which she refused.

She may as well have been on medication, the way she felt the next few days. Sharp, stabbing grief one moment, lightheaded nothingness the next. Overwhelming fatigue and mental fuzziness as she battled to take care of things: Notify neighbors and friends. Write an obituary. Order a casket. Plan a funeral.

Carrie stopped in her walk down F Street. Memories of Grandma's death had stirred her so deeply that tears had slipped onto her cheeks. She fumbled in her skirt pocket for a handkerchief and blotted her face. A feeling of empathy for Nate rose in her heart as she recognized that her experience qualified her to know what he was going through and what he might face.

Nate needed her. She must go to him. Whether it would be appropriate or not, Carrie didn't know or care. All that mattered is that she wanted to be with him during this difficult time.

Carrie started walking again, this time with purpose.

Chapter Thirty-six

During dinner, Carrie updated the Owenses on Mr. Landon's condition. As they talked, the idea came to her that she could ride home with Nate every afternoon when he finished work and help with dinner preparations and household chores. She immediately voiced her plan.

"Helen has her own family to care for, and if she's spending most of the day with James' parents, she's not going to be able to keep up with her own work."

As Bertie passed a platter of fried chicken, she looked at Carrie. "That's a very generous thought. Do you think you can do class preparations, grade papers, and have time to spend evenings with the Landons?"

"I'll work as hard as I can from the time classes dismiss in the afternoon, until five or six in the evening."

Mr. Owens speared a piece of chicken and put it on his plate. "I'm wondering how Nate will take to this idea?"

Carrie smiled. "He won't. I'll have to warm him up to it."

"I bet," Mr. Owens said. "Nate is a young man with a lot of pride, but you are a persuasive young woman." He wiped a napkin across his mouth as he chuckled. "I'm so curious to see how things come about that I'll make you an offer."

"What's that?" Carrie asked.

"I'll drive you over there this evening to see if this plan can be launched."

By 7 p.m., Carrie was knocking on the Landons' front door while Mr. Owens waited in his car. When Nate opened, he stepped back in surprise. "Carrie, what are you doing here?"

She grinned and launched into her plan for helping him and his family. As she expected, he resisted, until she suggested they give it a try for only a day or two.

Nate stood aside and motioned her in. "Come in, Carrie. I'll speak to Mr. Owens and tell him to go on. I'll drive you home later."

For the next half hour, Carrie and Nate visited with his parents in their room. Mr. Landon sat up in his bed, looking and sounding healthy for a man of his age and condition. Briefly, Carrie wondered if he might be the age of her father, had he lived, a thought that convinced her of the rightness of what she was doing.

Mr. Landon seemed to enjoy the conversation, asking Carrie what she liked about teaching and where she took her training.

"Chicago Normal School. I was inspired by a former principal of the school, Ella Flagg Young. She was the first woman in America to head a large city school system."

"Is that so?" Mr. Landon asked.

"Yes. The woman was amazing. I totally idolized her."

Mrs. Landon reached for her husband's hand while she looked at Carrie and Nate. "It's been lovely talking with you both. I think William needs to rest, now."

"Oh, I'm sorry if I talked too much," Carrie said.

"It's alright, Carrie, You didn't talk too much," Nate assured her. "Mom is very protective of Dad."

"And for good reason," Carrie replied as she stepped closer to the bed. "I've really enjoyed visiting with you, Mr. Landon, and I'm praying you're soon well."

"Thank you," Mr. Landon smiled. "Come again, won't you?"

Nate ushered Carrie from the room, across the living room and into the kitchen. "You're not in a hurry to go home, I hope." He pulled a chair out for her at the table. "I thought we might talk a little bit."

She sat down and he sat across from her. "What do you think about my father's condition?"

"He looks good, Nate. Better than I expected. And he's a wonderful man. I'm praying for him."

"Prayer. Isn't that something new for you, Carrie?"

Carrie dropped her eyes for a minute, then looked up. "Like I said before, the flood has changed my thinking about a lot of things." She leaned forward in her chair, placing her hands on the table. "I'm not mad at God anymore. I don't understand why bad things happen, but I know I need Him to be with me. Like I need you. In all kinds of situations." She took a deep breath. "And you need me."

Nate reached across the table for her hands and held them tightly. "I've been thinking the same thing," he said, his voice quiet and low.

They sat that way for several minutes. Carrie thought he might say more, but he didn't. Instead, he caressed her hands in his. Finally, he spoke. "There's so much going on in my life right now, Carrie. I can't make any promises."

"You don't have to. Let's just work through this—together."

"I'd like that," he said.

Carrie smiled, scooted her chair back and stood. "Right now, I'd say there's some work to do in this kitchen." Her eyes scanned the room, landing on the sink full of dirty dishes.

"Sorry for the mess," Nate immediately apologized. "Helen didn't have time—"

"That's the point of my visit. I'm here to help. Now, find me an apron."

Nate picked an apron off a peg on the wall of the pantry and handed it to her. He stayed beside her as she cleared the sink, filled it with hot water, added soap and started washing the dishes. He dried and put them away. When they finished, they looked at each other. A half-smile crept onto Nate's face. "Is this what you call 'working together'?"

Carrie grinned back at him. "You're a fast learner."

He hugged her, and she whispered in his ear. "I think you'd better take me home because there'll be a whole classroom of children waiting for me in the morning to help them be fast learners."

After notifying his parents, Nate drove Carrie home. As they neared F Street, Carrie asked, "Day one of our experiment. Do we continue tomorrow? Will you pick me up when you get off work?"

"I sure enjoyed this evening. I think we should try another day of it."

"Good. Remember, I'll be coming to help. If there are any chores you need done...."

Nate stopped the truck in front of the Owenses' house. "I'll have a list so long, you'll wish you never signed up for this." He smiled as he helped her out of the car and walked her to the door.

"Hurry home," Carrie said. "I don't want your parents to be alone any longer than absolutely necessary."

"Trying to run me off," Nate laughed as he kissed her cheek.

She watched him walk toward his truck and wave as he drove away. When she opened the door, Mr. Owens was turning off the floor lamp next to his chair. "Just heading for bed," he said. "How'd it go?"

"Well enough that we'll give it another try tomorrow."

Chapter Thirty-seven

For ten days, Carrie spent evenings at the Landons', fixing meals, cleaning up the kitchen, and visiting. Her good deeds tired her more than she expected, since she had to keep up with her school work, as well. The bonus was spending time with Nate and getting to know his parents. His father was a friendly man who enjoyed conversing on a wide range of topics. His mother was more reserved, though she expressed her opinions quite strongly at times. It seemed to Carrie that Mrs. Landon was still evaluating her, while Mr. Landon accepted her.

The driving time to and from the Landons' home is what Carrie valued most. It couldn't have taken more than fifteen minutes each way, enough time to share the events of their days, insufficient time to cover major topics. Nate chatted happily about his job at the lumber and hardware stores. He was earning sixteen cents an hour. He also had ongoing repair jobs. which made him more and more certain that he could build a business of his own some day.

Carrie encouraged him in his dreams.

Meanwhile, Mr. Landon's health improved. After a week of total bed rest, the doctor allowed him to walk as far as the living room and sit in his favorite chair. Before long, he had ventured to the kitchen to take his meals at the table. The beginning of March brought seventy-degree weather and sunshine. Mr. and Mrs. Landon sat on the front porch for short periods of time in the afternoons.

They no longer needed as much household help. Helen came for two hours every morning, and Carrie came only on weekend evenings. It left a vacuum in her life, though she was grateful to get back to a more normal schedule with her teaching responsibilities.

One Saturday evening, as Carrie and Nate sat in the living room visiting with his parents, his father suddenly interrupted them by saying, "You two don't need to sit around with us old folks any more. Why don't you get out and go somewhere, just the two of you?"

Nate looked at Carrie, a smile spreading across his face. "Where would you like to go?"

"I don't know," she stammered. "I'm so used to our present schedule that I haven't thought of anything else."

Nate's father pulled out his pocket watch. "It's only seven thirty."

"That settles it," Nate said as he stood up. "Let's be on our way, Carrie. We'll figure out a destination as we go along."

Minutes later, Nate and Carrie had their coats on and were walking out the door.

"Have a good time!" Mr. Landon called after them.

"Is your father scheming to get us together?" Carrie asked as they walked toward Nate's truck.

"He likes you, Carrie."

"What about your mother? She seems a little uncertain about me."

"Oh, I'm sure Mom likes you, too. You know how mothers are. They think there's no one good enough for their sons. She was like that when James and Helen married. Now she thinks the sun rises and sets in Helen."

Nate helped Carrie into the truck, dashed around to the driver's seat, started the engine and headed down the driveway. Carrie peered out the windshield at the shapes of lemon trees in the darkness as they passed groves on either side of the road.

"I wish I had a family for you to meet," she said in a small voice. "Grandma would have liked you, I'm sure."

Nate patted Carrie's hand but said nothing.

"She didn't like Tony," Carrie continued.

"Who's Tony?" Nate asked as he glanced her direction.

"A man in Chicago who wanted to marry me. Grandma kept telling me he was not the one for me."

"Am I in competition with this man?" Nate asked. "It's not surprising that a woman like you would have many offers for marriage."

"No. It's over. I learned the truth about Tony."

Nate guided the truck onto Third Avenue. All the stores and shops were closed. He drove to the end of the two-block business district, turned left and came up on the back side of the church. He parked the truck on the edge of the street.

"Nothing's open, and I can't think of anyplace to go, so we might as well sit here and you can tell me the rest of the story about Tony."

Carrie sighed. "I've been wanting to."

"Go ahead, Carrie. I'm listening, and whatever you tell me won't change how I feel about you."

"It was a few days after Grandma's funeral. I was clearing out her apartment and came across some papers in her desk."

Carrie held up the yellowed newspaper dated December 15, 1898. Halfway down the page, a headline had been circled. It read "Pedestrian killed by car." Her eyes dropped to the opening line of the story. "While walking home from work, Mr. John Wyngate—"

Carrie caught her breath. Her hands began to shake and she dropped the paper on the floor. "Daddy!"

Her mind immediately took her to the evening when Grandma told her that Daddy wasn't coming home. Carrie was only five years old, but the memories were as clear as though it happened yesterday.

She picked up the newspaper clipping and continued reading. "It was twilight. The street lights had just been lit. Mr. Wyngate stepped off the curb at Third and Grover Avenues. A large, black vehicle swept around the corner, striking—"

Tears sprang to Carrie's eyes and she brushed them away with her fingers so she could continue reading. "Witnesses say the driver was at fault. Police identified him as Johnny Mancini."

Carrie gasped. "Mancini? Could he be related to Tony Mancini? My Tony?"

"Was he?" Nate asked.

Carrie turned toward Nate and stared at him, not seeing him. She shook her head and blinked her eyes, the memories so vivid, she didn't know whether she was there or here. Finally, her mind brought her to the present.

"Yes. Johnny was Tony's uncle."

"What a shock that must have been."

"A terrible shock. It turned out the Mancini family had ties with the mafia, too. How close, I didn't find out. Another newspaper clipping that Grandma saved said that Johnny Mancini would likely be tried for the death of my father because witnesses all said he was driving recklessly. There was also the hint that he might have been carrying out a mafia revenge errand at the time. But there never was a trial."

"Are you sure?" Nate crinkled his eyebrows together.

"A page in Grandma's diary—another item I found in her desk—written in her handwriting. The Mancini family apparently bought off the authorities. There will be no trial. There is no justice. Grandma underlined the last two words, no justice. Then she wrote a Bible verse, which will be stuck in my head forever: Judgment is turned away backward and justice standeth afar off: for truth is fallen in the street. Isaiah 59:14."

"Whoo-o-o-o-o." Nate expelled a breath as he leaned back in his seat and clasped his hands behind his neck, then dropped them and turned to face Carrie. "What a thing to discover."

"That's when I decided to leave Chicago. I could not marry into a family that caused the death of my father."

"What did Tony say about that?"

"I didn't tell him. I didn't tell anyone. I just left. And came here."

"That took courage," Nate said quietly.

"It scared me so much. It still scares me. I'm sure Grandma wouldn't have let me marry Tony. She would have told me. If she hadn't died suddenly."

Nate put his finger under Carrie's chin, turning her face toward his and looked directly into her eyes. "I'm sorry you went through all that."

"Me, too. What bothers me is that sometimes I worry that he, or some of their clan, might come looking for me." Carrie dropped her head and clutched her hands together.

Nate put his hands over hers and said, "I don't think they'd do that. They probably have bigger fish to fry, as the saying goes."

"I was very careful not to leave any clues as to where I was going. I didn't even tell my best friend, Rose." Carrie sniffled. "She probably thinks some awful thing happened to me. I've wanted so much to write to her, but I'm afraid."

Nate caressed Carrie's hands. "You've been carrying a big bundle of worries." He looked into her eyes as a lopsided smile formed at the corner of his mouth. "If it's any comfort to you, I'd run off the whole Mancini clan if they showed up in Chula Vista."

Carrie attempted a smile. "You don't know how much safer that makes me feel." Lifting a finger to her eye, she brushed away the moisture dampening her lashes. "Actually, I'm feeling better than I have in a long time. I think it's helped to talk about it."

Nate pulled her close to him, and they sat together looking through the darkness at the backside of the church. Suddenly, Nate hit the steering wheel with his left fist and blurted, "By Jove, Carrie, this is no place to be spending an evening with a beautiful woman like you. We should be in a nice restaurant somewhere or strolling through a park. I bet you had lots of places like that in Chicago. Look at this town. Two blocks of businesses— all of them shut up tight at five p.m. Nothing to do around here. No way to get out of here, either, what with the flood damage to the bridges and railroad tracks."

Carrie shrugged. "At least we're together."

"I know. But I want to take you somewhere special."

"I'm sure things will get back to normal soon and we can get out and do something different."

Nate took his arm from Carrie's shoulder and leaned forward, his hands against the steering wheel. "Maybe I'm over-reacting to all that we've been through the last few weeks. The flood. The loss of lives. Destruction of property. Dad's illness. Even that was a result of the flood." Nate turned his face toward Carrie. "Did you know there are a number of people who are leaving town? They say they've had enough."

"I heard that. You're not one of them, though."

"No." Nate tightened his fingers around the steering wheel, then released them and looked at her. "How do you know me so well?"

Carrie laughed. "I've been studying you for awhile."

"And what have you learned?"

"That something good came out of the flood. You. Us."

Nate bent toward her and kissed her forehead, her nose, her cheeks, her chin and finally, her lips. Full. Warm. Passionately.

Several minutes later, she eased away from him. "I think it's about time I turn in for the night. Would you mind driving me home?"

Nate pulled back, stroking her hair with his fingers before he put his hand on the gear shift. "I'd drive you anywhere in the world that you wanted to go," he said. "As long as I could come along."

His sly grin made her heart jump, and she half wondered if he heard it thumping against her chest wall. Carrie leaned her head backward against the seat and closed her eyes for a second, letting her body relax while her heart skipped like a school girl jumping rope.

The truck bumped along the rutted street until they reached the Owenses' home. Holding her hand, Nate walked Carrie to the door, saying, "As soon as the railroad is operating again, I want to take you to San Diego for a whole day. Or maybe Coronado. We'll see the sights. Dine at a good restaurant."

"That'd be nice, Nate."

Chapter Thirty-eight

Nate couldn't sleep that night. Worries kept rising in his mind. He knew what he wanted to do, but facts and figures kept getting in the way. In his head, he multiplied his wages by tentative hours to find how long it would take to.... Too long.

He added on the sum of his savings account and remembered there were still several months of expenses to deduct before the lemon crop could be harvested. Who knew if he'd clear anything in that venture. Too uncertain.

The promise Nate had made to himself about Carrie danced like an elusive ghost just beyond his reach. He finally fell asleep with the sheets and blankets twisted around his sweaty body. The sun shone full strength into his room when he half-opened his eyes the following morning. Blinking, he looked at the clock on the dresser. Eight o'clock. I'll be late for work. As he untangled himself from the bedding, it came to him that it was Sunday.

Three hours later, Nate sat in the Landon pew at church. His parents were not with him, adhering to the doctor's prescription of two more weeks of quiet before William could go out. Nate didn't see Carrie and twisted his neck two or three times until he spotted her sitting four rows behind him. It's funny how knowing she's there makes me feel good.

When the service ended, Nate walked in Carrie's direction, only to be stopped by Mr. Greenley, a well-muscled railroad worker for many decades and a friend of his father. Quickly, Nate updated the man on his father's health.

"Glad he's doing better," Mr. Greenley said as he unbuttoned his suit coat and took a deep breath. "I always feel like a sausage about to split its casing in these clothes."

Nate smiled and glanced in Carrie's direction, hoping she wouldn't leave before he got to her.

"By the way, Nate, I've got some good news about the railroad."

Nate directed his eyes to Mr. Greenley again.

"We're nearly finished with the bridge repairs. The electric train is going to be ready to operate by the middle of the week."

"Great! I can't wait to take an out-of-town trip." Nate glanced again in Carrie's direction. "Thanks, Mr. Greenley, for the good news. Now, if you'll excuse me...."

"Certainly, Nate. Give your father my regards."

Nate was already moving toward Carrie, trying to walk nonchalantly but wanting to run to her before she got too far away. She had left the main group of chatting parishioners and was ready to turn onto F Street. He came up behind her. "Carrie, wait."

She pirouetted and faced him, her eyes shaded by a wide-brimmed, ivory-colored hat with a green feather in it. Her lips were slightly parted, the corners drawn up in a smile. A breeze ruffled a curl next to her face, and she raised a kid-gloved hand to smooth it in place.

She looks like a goddess and I feel like a clown. Nate stepped back and stammered "Uh... uh...the railroad's starting up again."

Carrie cocked her head and raised her eyebrows.

"Repairs on the railroad are nearly done. They'll be open for business the middle of the week."

"Oh." Carrie looked confused.

"Which means we can take that trip to San Diego or Coronado." Nate stepped closer. "How about next Saturday?"

"That'd be perfect."

The following week, three incidents occurred that reassured Nate about his plans. On Monday when he reported for work at the lumber yard and hardware store, both proprietors said that business was brisk and they'd need Nate for at least twenty hours each week, possibly more, on a permanent basis.

On Tuesday, the widow Covington pressed $2 in his hand. "Sorry it's taken me so long to pay you for fixing my fence last summer."

Thursday, one of the homeowners of a flood-damaged house, paid him $4 for repairs.

Nate claimed these events as omens of good things to come and planned what he would say and do on Saturday.

The warm March weather made children wiggle in their school desks, challenging all of Carrie's skills to keep them focused on learning. By the middle of the week, she felt exhausted and longed for the weekend. She had not been out of Chula Vista since December. In her earlier years, Carrie had never traveled far from Chicago, but it had so much more to offer: large department stores, cozy cafes, lavish restaurants, museums, art galleries, concert halls, parks. Suddenly, she missed it all. If anyone had told her a year earlier that she'd be living in a tiny town known only for its lemons, she would have laughed.

Her memories gave her pause as she considered that she was on the verge of committing herself to a lifetime in this spot on the western edge of the continent. That is, if Nate proposed. She didn't think it would happen soon, not with the financial goals she knew he had set for himself.

Thinking about Nate jerked her back to present realities and caused her to shake off the wave of homesickness that had snuck upon her. There was nothing for her in Chicago, and everything for her in Chula Vista.

Carrie turned her mind to planning what to wear on Saturday.

It was cloudy on Saturday morning. Carrie dressed in a blue suit with long, belted jacket which she left unbuttoned at the top to display an ivory-colored blouse with lace-edged collar beneath. Her hat, a straight-brimmed one, matched the suit. Carrie played with different angles for the hat placement, settling on a slight tip to the right. She pulled on a pair of white gloves and carried a small drawstring bag.

Nate met her at the Owenses' front door, dressed in a light brown suit and carrying a hat in his hand.

"You don't usually wear a hat," Carrie remarked.

"I'm not wearing it now," Nate joked. "Hats bother me, and I'm always losing them, so I generally don't wear one. Today is a special day, though." He placed the hat on his head.

"Looks good on you."

Nate offered her his arm, and they walked toward the electric train stop on Third Avenue where a long line of people stood.

"Looks like everyone in Chula Vista decided to leave town today," Carrie said.

Within minutes, the train pulled in, stopped, and everyone pushed forward. There were more people than seats, so Nate stood. When the train left Chula Vista and crossed the Sweetwater River, Carrie kept her eyes on the window. Flood damage was still very evident, with debris of all kinds thrown onto the banks of the river on either side. Uprooted trees, brush, planks, boards, even an intact chicken coop littered the edges of the river. A water line, many feet above the current level of the river, marked the height of the flood.

Everyone on the train stared and commented: "Can you believe the water got that high?" "It's a wonder there weren't more casualties." "Hope we don't see the likes of that again." "Mr. Hatfield's formulas worked too well."

A tall gentleman standing behind Nate asked in a loud voice, "How many people want to sue Mr. Hatfield?" Many hands popped up, and a discussion broke loose about the fact that the city of San Diego had already been sued. The same tall man dominated the talk. "The city will never pay. They claim it wasn't their fault. It was Hatfield's. He's not going to own the responsibility."

A chorus of grumbles filled the car as people complained about the unfairness of it all. Nate leaned down to Carrie and whispered in her ear, "Shall I break this negative spell by telling everybody how the flood helped us?"

Carrie grinned. "Let's keep that little secret to ourselves."

As the electric train moved north through National City, more storm damage came into view. Rutted streets, mud-spattered buildings, fallen trees. The tracks snaked along a roadbed barely cleared enough to the width of the train. Even in downtown San Diego with its paved streets, there were traces of powdery dried mud on the sidewalks and parks where the grass was still flattened. Carrie looked up to Nate, who stood behind her. "It's pretty amazing that they got the train up and running this fast, considering all the damage we've been seeing."

Nate nodded. "We'll be getting off in a few minutes at the Santa Fe station. If you don't mind, I thought we'd go directly to Coronado, rather than staying in the city."

"You're my tour guide. I'll go wherever you take me." Carrie smiled, folded her hands in her lap and watched the passing cityscape of hotels, theatres, and department stores. People crowded the sidewalks. Cars and horse-drawn carts filled the streets.

They exited the train at the Santa Fe station. Carrie remembered going through it in August when a train from the east deposited her at this spot and she transferred to the electric train to Chula Vista. A high graceful arch at the entry of the station invited travelers inside to a large room with high ceilings of natural redwood beams. An eight and a half foot high wainscoting of green, yellow, blue and white tiles in a Moorish design edged with ziggurats lined the walls. Long oak benches stretched the length of the room. Carrie and Nate spent a few minutes admiring the building and the patio area decorated with potted flowers and palms.

"It's a beautiful building for a train station," Carrie remarked.

"Brand new. Just opened last year," Nate explained.

"I like the Spanish-style architecture. We didn't have anything like that in Chicago."

Nate pointed westward to the bay. "We'll walk a couple of blocks to the harbor and catch the ferry."

The clouds were beginning to break apart, letting sunlight through to dance on the waters of the bay. A few sailboats skimmed over the surface, keeping a respectful distance from a large cargo ship moving slowly up the bay.

When they reached the waterfront, Nate and Carrie boarded the Coronado ferry, a small boat, which took them across the bay. They sat together on an outside deck looking at the skyline of San Diego. "It's quite an impressive city from this view," Nate said.

"It is," Carrie agreed. "When I first heard of San Diego, I thought it was just a little wild-west town, but it isn't. It looks important."

"We've attracted a lot of attention and visitors with the Panama Exposition. You remember going there that Saturday night not long after you came here?"

"Of course I remember. I got jealous of the way Mary flirted with you."

"You did?" Nate reached for her hand and twined his fingers around hers. "I thought you didn't want anything to do with me."

"I didn't, but I didn't want anyone else to have you, either."

Nate shook his head. "No wonder I was confused."

In less than twenty minutes, the ferry crossed the bay and pulled alongside a wharf. Nate and Carrie disembarked and stepped into a trolley that took them to the del Coronado Hotel on the opposite side of the island.

Carrie saw the hotel long before they reached it. It's red-roofed dome dominated the sky. The trolley stopped on a nearby street. Nate and Carrie walked a short way and entered a wide driveway curving upward to the main entrance of the hotel. Long, low steps, lined by potted plants, led to the doorway. A doorman, dressed in red jacket and cap, opened the door with a white-gloved hand. Inside, the mahogany-paneled entry opened into a domed reception area.

Carrie stood in the middle of the room, looking around and upward. Rich, dark woodwork covered everything. There were several large doors around the room. "Those lead into ballrooms and dining rooms." Nate explained. "Let's take a peek inside." He reached for a door handle and opened it. Linen-covered tables with fresh-flower centerpieces filled the room. The far wall was all glass, floor-to-ceiling windows opening onto a vista of the Pacific Ocean.

"Oh!" Carrie said. "Isn't that beautiful!"

"We'll eat dinner here, later," Nate said. "I made reservations."

Carrie didn't know why she felt surprised at Nate. He isn't just a small-town boy, she thought. He knows how to do things with style. She took hold of his arm, and he looked down at her and grinned.

"Does that suit you, Mademoiselle?"

"Absolutely."

"Let's go outside," Nate said as he guided her out of the dining room, through the reception room and into a large courtyard. Two stories of hotel rooms wrapped themselves around the courtyard. They followed a path that eventually led them to the other side of the hotel to grassy lawns, tennis courts and a boardwalk that skirted the beach. Hand in hand, they walked the boardwalk, the magnificent hotel beside them on one side, the beach and the ocean on the other. The surf rolled in gently, crashing softly onto the white sand, making it glisten with wetness.

"I want to walk on the beach," Carrie said.

Minutes later, they had taken off their shoes, stashed them under a log and run toward the water. Carrie squealed when her toes hit the water. "Oooh! That's cold!" She backed up, nearly knocking Nate over as he ran up behind her. He grabbed her around the waist and spun her about. They threw their heads back, laughing together. Carrie's hat slid off, and Nate caught it. They retraced their steps to the log, set their hats down, covering them with their jackets.

Nate rolled up his pant legs, and once again, they bolted to the water's edge. This time, Carrie ran into the surf up to her ankles. Nate followed. They stopped and stood still, letting waves wash up over their feet, then watching them recede in fast-moving ripples. A breeze tousled their hair, the sun shone on their upturned faces. So much happiness filled Carrie that she thought she'd explode.

She smiled at Nate, and in that second, a bigger wave hit her legs at calf-height. She stumbled, and Nate caught her, but not before the hem of her skirt dipped into the water. Carrie looked down. "Oh dear, my skirt is wet. My hair is blown about. How can I go to dinner in a fancy place looking like this?"

Nate drew her closer to himself. "You look beautiful." He dropped his eyes. "I especially like your bare toes."

Carrie swatted his arm. "You big tease."

"I'm not teasing. Those are the cutest toes I've ever seen."

Heat rose from Carrie's neck to her face and she giggled.

They walked back to the log, sat down and waited for their feet to dry. Carrie leaned into Nate, and he put his arm around her. They watched clouds form and re-shape themselves over the ocean, then scatter into thin strips of vapor. Gulls rode air waves above the water, while tiny sandpipers skittered about in the shallows. A woman strolled across the sand, bending over from time to time to pick up a shell or rock and pocket it. Ahead of her, a man walked briskly, with a dog on a leash beside him.

"It's peaceful here," Carrie whispered. "I think I'd like to live in a house next to the beach."

"You'd prefer a beach house to an orchard house?"

Carrie shrugged. "It depends."

"Depends on what?"

"Who I'm with."

Nate sat very still, keeping his eyes straight ahead, studying the ocean. Finally, he turned toward Carrie. "Lately, I've been thinking a lot about who I want to be with."

He paused, and Carrie kept still as she wondered where this conversation was going. Nate stayed quiet so long, she decided it wasn't going anywhere. Finally, he spoke. "When I first met you last summer, Carrie, I was attracted to you. I guess you didn't feel the same about me."

"I did, Nate. I did. I was just too scared to admit it."

"Are you still scared, Carrie?"

"No. That all changed when I thought I'd lost you in the flood, and then I found you."

"Good, because I really want us to continue to be together." Nate cleared his throat. "The timing is all wrong. The flood. The lemon crop. I don't even know if there'll be a crop. Or if I'll make money or lose money."

Carrie felt Nate's hand tighten against her shoulder.

"Then there's my dad." Nate sighed. "There are so many uncertainties."

"There always have been and always will be," Carrie replied.

"I know. Life is never perfect," Nate said. "But I'd like it to be a little better for you than what I can offer."

Carrie held her breath and closed her eyes. While her heart wished for one thing, her head told her that Nate would not say what she'd like him to say. Not now. She'd have to wait. It was alright. As long as he didn't go away. Panic suddenly filled her chest like thunderclouds rising in a summer sky. He wouldn't break off their friendship, would he? He was lifting his arm from her shoulder, moving away. She was terrified. Her eyes opened just as Nate slipped to one knee.

He took both her hands in his, looked into her eyes and said, "Carrie,

I've come to love you so much that I can't imagine life without you." He cleared his throat. "So, Miss Carolyn Wyngate, will you marry me?"

"Yes!" Carrie squealed.

Nate pulled her to himself, embracing her so tightly it almost squeezed the breath out of her. She felt her heart pounding in her ears as she tipped her head back. Everything slowed, his face bending toward hers, their lips meeting, the kiss long and warm. Carrie's fingers tightened around his neck. Eventually, she opened her eyes and mumbled, "I think people are staring at us."

"I don't care," Nate said. "On the other hand, perhaps this is a good time to give you something."

He thrust his hand in his pocket and withdrew it again. Whatever he held, it was small because his hand concealed it completely. Gradually, he unfolded his fingers and she saw a wooden heart in his palm. He held it out to her.

Carrie took it, the sheen of highly polished wood smooth beneath her touch. "You made this, didn't you?"

"Yes. It's really not much. I plan to buy an engagement ring, but want you to help select it. Besides, you've noticed that we don't have a jewelry store in Chula Vista, and we haven't had transportation to San Diego until now. So I decided to make something for you for this special occasion."

"It's wonderful!" Carrie turned it over. "You carved our initials on it. Oh, Nate, you couldn't buy me anything as special as this. I'll cherish it forever."

"That's good, because I bought a chain so you could wear it around your neck." He fished in another pocket and withdrew a long, silver chain, which he threaded through a hole in the wooden heart. Then he fastened it around her neck. "Maybe that's too much with the locket you're already wearing."

Carrie reached behind her neck, unhooked the chain carrying her locket, removed it and dropped it into her purse. "I'll put the locket away in a special place with my old memories. I'll wear your heart from now on because we're making new memories together."

They kissed again, then sat scrunched into each other on the log, watching cloud shadows and sunlight play hopscotch across the surface of the ocean. They talked of the future.

"You realize, of course," Carrie said, "that you're not getting a country girl. I don't know how to milk a cow, ride a horse, kill a chicken or even pluck it."

Nate's eyes grew round. "You don't? Then the deal's off." He threw his head back and laughed. "You've noticed, haven't you, that Chula Vista has a butcher shop? Besides that, our town is not going to stay a tiny rural community. It's going to be a real city. You and I are going to have a part in making it a wonderful place for families to live and grow up together."

He laughed again. "So, Miss Carolyn Wyngate, soon to be Mrs. Carolyn Landon, we're going ahead with our plans even if you can't pluck a chicken. A city girl is exactly what I want."

Sequel

While gathering critiques and making revisions, it came to several of my readers and myself that a sequel begs to be written to When Rain Comes. There's more to be told about Carrie and Nate, intriguing plot lines to follow, secrets to disclose, an evil character to conquer, young love that needs strengthening.

Yep. You guessed it. I'm already working on the next story. You can follow my progress at my blog or Facebook page. Better yet, sign up for e-mail notices. Be a test reader. Help pick a title for the next book.

Send me an e-mail and ask to be on a list for regular updates: patgmaxwell@gmail.com.

Follow me on the journey toward publication of a sequel:

webpage and blog: www.patriciagmaxwell.com

Facebook: www.facebook.com/patricia.g.maxwell.7